the reason why

the reason why

A Novel By

Nicole McKay

Published by Nikki McKay Enterprises

Cover and Interior Design by TWA Solutions.com

ISBN: 978-0-9894941-0-6

 Library of Congress Control Number: 2013910324

Printed in the United States of America

Acknowledgments

Lord, I thank You for loving me even when I gave mere man more authority in my life than I gave You. Thank You God for deliverance!

Tiffany, JT and AJ, I thank you. You have been my inspiration as I looked at your pictures to propel and motivate me to keep writing. Ma, Daddy, Celeste, James, Lester, Russell and John Jr., I thank you. Living with you all has been an integral part of my journey.

Thank you to all of my friends and family. It's just too many of you to name, but know that I love you all and thank you!

Finally, I want to thank Erica, Andrea, Anthony, John, Kiara, Tarren, Strad, Justin and Christine for bringing *The Reason Why* to life on the stage. I love you all!

Chapter 1

"*Damn*, girl…shit…don't beat it, suck it."

Nadia tried not to roll her eyes or look agitated, as she stopped mercilessly yanking his dick, trying to detach it, which seemed to be the only recourse she had for the nightly sex sessions with Steve, her husband, of nearly ten years.

Positioned between his thighs, Nadia desperately wanted the blowjob to end, as she struggled to gather enough saliva to slicken his ashy penis. Maybe it was a mind thing, but no matter how hard she tried, she couldn't conjure up enough spit to get the job done. And, he was starting to go limp.

Hell nah, she thought. *I have to get this thing back up or this session will never end!*

That thought must have been all she needed, as Nadia's mouth instantly filled with enough saliva to slob two knobs. It's amazing what the mind can do.

Wetting him from tip to balls, Nadia exhaled, sucking slowly while looking at the clock.

Ten-fifty-two.

Deep within, her frustration grew as her jaws tightened. *This is some bullshit!* Hated it! She simply hated pleasing his ass on all levels.

By ten fifty-seven, the Sandman should make his appearance, and she should be done and in sleepy land by exactly eleven. It was going to happen, as determination and exhaustion were her motivating factors.

Begrudgingly, with her mouth wrapped around his shaft, her head bobbed up and down. Her strokes were rough and forceful. Determination is something else.

His body tensed. *There ya go,* she thought; she had him. *Come on, motherfucker!*

Steve wound her hair into a tight fist. "Ahhh…girl, that's it," Steve groaned, bobbing her head up and down. "Suck Daddy's dick, baby." His thighs tensed; his toes pointed like a ballerina. "Faster, baby. Faster!"

You want fast? I'll give your ass fast, and that she did! Nadia was like a locomotive on warp speed. If she stroked him any faster, she'd peel the skin clean off.

The last thing she wanted was for her husband to enjoy this moment. It was total work for her and she was ready to resign.

After a few minutes of sucking, her hand took over, vigorously beating his dick, *again.* As she moved his meat up and down, he was becoming dry, *again*; nothing but friction. She didn't care. She wanted him to hurt, acting like she had no clue about the torture she was putting him through. There were times she hated him so much she wanted to have his third leg walking on crutches. It's a dangerous thing for a man to want his precious jewel in the mouth of a woman he has mistreated.

It's ten-fifty-four, and in forty-five seconds Nadia was going to speed up the intensity and beat that motherfucker 'til it damn near killed him.

From the look on Steve's face, he was in pain and his semen was building up, too; the bulging veins told her so. His eyes rolled up in his head with pleasure, while grimacing.

She looked at him, playing the seduction role and loving this whipping she was putting on him. Was it possible that Steve was enjoying this pain? Possibly, but she had to try to do something. She premeditated this calculated beat down, so that maybe he would leave her alone for the rest of the night and she could get a few hours of sleep. The next morning would start a busy day, and she needed all the rest she could get.

Ten-fifty-six...

The countdown to ending this beating was on.

"Oooh...damn...girl...ouch!"

Beat it, kill it, destroy it, yank it, yank it!

"I'm coming!" he groaned, eyes rolling back in his head.

Yes! It's over!

Ten-fifty-seven. Perfect timing.

"How did that feel, baby?" she asked, releasing his now shriveled manhood.

Steve massaged himself. "Girl, what were you trying to do? Make sure we never have sex again?"

Steve looked very uncomfortable and he looked at her suspiciously. He sat up for a few seconds and moved to the edge of the bed. Never taking his eyes off her, he looked somewhat confused before he got out of bed and went into the bathroom of their master bedroom.

Damn right, she thought, but wouldn't dare say it out loud. She had to find a way to cope with Steve's aggressive, sexual appetite and if he had a clue about what she just did to get back at him for how he forced sex on her, he would kill her.

Hurriedly, she found her panties, which had been tossed on the floor, and put them on. Maybe her panties and his mutilated penis would serve as a deterrent for a second session tonight. All she could do was hope for the best.

Hearing the toilet flush and running water from the sink faucet, she climbed in bed and pulled the comforter up around her neck, pretending to be asleep. Even if she and Steve had a marathon sex session, he would always have energy for a second round. Prior to this round, they had sex an hour before and, yet, he needed more, which is why she decided to blow him. She just didn't want her husband inside her anymore. She tried to yank his dick hard enough for him to be in too much agony to come at her again. She was still fearful, though, that he would ignore the pain.

Having to be up at four-thirty in the morning, she was totally exhausted. She really hoped Steve would be exhausted, too, but she already knew the chances of that were slim to none.

Turning off the faucet, Steve opened the bathroom door and she breathed a heavy sigh, trying to give her best fake-sleeping performance. He lifted the burnt orange, silk comforter and climbed in close, spooning her. He nuzzled his face in her neck, and then kissed her ear. His hand slid over her belly, inching down to her panties.

Damn, this fool is really coming at me again! This shit is ridiculous. I have to get some rest or I won't be any good tomorrow, she thought, growing more agitated by his very touch.

How could this be possible? After what Nadia put him through, he was ready, *again.* She didn't have the strength, let alone the energy to do another hour of humping and pumping. Doubting if she could even get wet, and he would just be pumping until he came, she had nothing left to give him. Nothing.

Nadia continued to breathe heavily and Steve continued to ease his finger into her panties. Realizing she had to do something, she moved Steve's hand and sat up.

"Steve, I really can't do any more tonight. I'm tired and I've been up all day. I have to get some rest," she pleaded, trying to give him her most pitiful, sleepy look.

Steve glared at Nadia. After a few seconds, he threw the comforter back, got out of bed and mumbled something about her being a nothing-ass bitch. He went in the bathroom for a second and returned with a towel wrapped around his waist. Then, he walked out of their bedroom, closing the door behind him.

"Not again," she mumbled.

Steve had a way of making Nadia feel guilty whenever she didn't do what he wanted her to do. She rarely told him no, but whenever she did, he would play her like a fiddle by ignoring her, knowing it drove her crazy.

Throwing back the covers, Nadia finally got out of bed, went to the closet, and got her robe. All she wanted to do was go to sleep and that seemed to be out of the question. She was going to fuck or argue tonight, and both required energy she couldn't muster. She opened the bedroom door and walked out into the living room. Steve was lying on the couch with his hands behind his head, staring at the ceiling.

Nadia sighed. She was so sick of his tantrums. "I'm sorry, Steve. I really want to make love to you tonight," she lied. "But I'm so tired."

Steve never took his eyes off the ceiling.

"I love you," she said.

Still, Steve said nothing.

Annoyed, Nadia shoved her hands in the pockets of her robe and returned to the bedroom. She sat on the edge of the bed. She knew all too well what was coming, and, damn it, she was tired of this dog and pony dance. Was this what her life had become? She didn't even know what the days of the week were sometimes because each day seemed to carry the same hurt and anguish.

Falling back on the bed, Nadia started feeling sorry for herself. For an hour, her mind raced about her life before she fell into an uneasy sleep.

She was lost.

Steve just couldn't seem to understand the sexual and emotional strain he placed on her daily. Couldn't he see that she was not a machine? And shit, even machines broke down, from time to time.

Throughout the night, Nadia woke up every twenty minutes or so with her heart beating out of her chest. Each time this happened, she would sit up, take deep breaths and count to ten. Then, she would try to pray. Truth be told, she was even tired of praying. If God hadn't heard and answered her prayers by now about her marriage, then maybe He just wasn't interested in what she had to say. Perhaps, with God, matters that are more important took precedence over her problems. There was a war being fought in Iraq. There were homeless people on the streets. The economy was a wreck. The murder rate was steadily climbing, and so on and so forth.

And then there was Nadia. Yes, she chose this life. The thought literally knotted her stomach. Had she sealed her destiny with God about her poor choice? Or did she need to become a better wife and make her household more harmonious? So, she figured she would stop bothering God, at least on this issue.

Hours later, she was awakened by the alarm clock. As she hit the alarm, an instant sadness came over her. She wanted to crawl deeper under the covers, rather than face the day. Anxious thoughts about her day and whatever form of mental punishment Steve felt she needed for denying him last night weighed heavily on her. She hated her life.

She sat up. It was chilly, so she pulled the comforter up to her neck. Her head was aching, and she needed some ibuprofen.

Listening intently, she heard Steve's footsteps approaching, which was odd because he never rose before her. Maybe he couldn't sleep either.

Steve entered the bedroom, the towel still wrapped around his waist, with a serious erection. He walked to his dresser drawer and retrieved a clean pair of underwear and an undershirt. Steve looked at her and she thought he was going to speak. Instead, the bitch in him took over and he walked out of the room without uttering a word. Once again, anxiety reared its ugly head, and she counted to ten to calm down.

Same shit, different day.

Chapter 2

Sitting up on the edge of the bed, it was four-thirty in the morning and Nadia contemplated hitting the treadmill. Her days were jammed packed, so getting up early to work out was the only time she had to exercise and clear her mind. She loved her alone time at the crack of dawn.

Nadia stood up, stretched her arms high above her head, scratched her butt and walked into the bathroom. Opening the medicine cabinet, she grabbed the bottle of ibuprofen, popped the top and shook the bottle, letting three tablets fall into the palm of her hand. Her head was killing her. She closed the cabinet door, and the image staring back at her looked a hot mess, with more bags than a bag lady and bloodshot eyes. She blinked a couple of times, as she almost didn't recognize herself, she looked so sad. After filling up the Dixie cup with water, and swallowing the pills, she didn't want to look at herself anymore, at least, not at that moment. Her reflection was depressing the hell out of her.

Nadia's early morning workout was what kept her going; the one thing she did for herself in her twenty-four-hour day. Theresa, her best friend, always joked about how she wished she had the discipline to get up early and exercise.

"Your ass is crazy as hell for getting up that early every damn morning. I wish I could do it," Theresa often said, laughing.

Theresa did work out though, but only after working all day and she would complain about getting home so late in the evening.

Nadia was grateful that staying motivated to work out had never been an issue for her. Perhaps her motivation comes from being involved in sports as a child, playing basketball and being on the cheerleading squad in grade school. Running track from grade school through high school didn't make her a star athlete. Moreover, she did develop discipline and maybe that gave her some form of mental patience. Often, she tried to think before reacting, but when she made a decision it was usually permanent, which was probably why she was so upset about the life she chose.

However, Nadia's life consisted of other areas where she definitely needed to be more disciplined, specifically with her finances. Emotional shopping was her saving grace. That is until she got home and checked the bank account. She would start at the mall, just looking. When she finally made a decision about the first thing she wanted and swiped that ATM card, it was on from that point, as she ended up buying stuff she really didn't need. Shopping was how she drowned her sorrows. And, she drowned herself in the process. She was in so much of a financial mess that she felt like she was sinking even further, with no kind of life preserver. One would think she would end this vicious cycle, but when her emotions were in overdrive, she would tell her logic to go to hell and followed her emotions.

For many, shopping was an addiction. But, for Nadia, it was an excuse to get out of the house and away from Steve.

Thinking back to when she ran track in high school, somehow Nadia managed to lose a fifty-yard lead, while running the mile relay. Each of the four-team members sprinted around the track once with a baton. At the end of each runner's lap, the baton was handed off to the next runner anxiously waiting to take off running toward the finish line, or the next runner. Usually, she ran third leg in the relay and preferred it. Third leg is considered the slowest leg of the four. The coach put his top speed at first and second leg to secure a good lead. Then, he would put his fastest person on fourth leg or anchor to make up whatever ground the third leg might have lost. For whatever reason, the coach decided that he would change up the line up at the championship track meet. *What type of foolishness was that?* The coach put the top speed runners at the first, second and third legs. Then, there was Nadia on anchor.

When the race started, Nadia stood on the side of the track hoping her team would not stay in first place. It wasn't that she wanted them to lose; she just didn't want them to lose because of her. Being the anchor carried a ton of pressure and she felt it, too.

To Nadia's utter dismay, it didn't happen like that at all. Their first leg blew by everybody like they were standing still, gaining a fifteen yard lead. The second leg had the audacity to stretch out the lead by ten additional yards. Her only hope was that the third leg would get burned, but unfortunately, that wasn't the case. As the third leg came down the stretch, getting ready to hand off the baton to her, it seemed as if they had the race in the bag.

"Go, go stick," the third leg sounded off, as she handed Nadia the baton.

When Nadia grabbed the baton, she ran for everything she was worth. She was running at a pace she knew would be impossible for her to maintain around the whole track, but she did it anyway. She made it around the first curve still out in the front. As she hit the backstretch, her breathing got heavier and her bottom lip was trembling. And, to make matters worse, it sounded like an army of tap shoes were behind her. That was the sound of the spikes on the shoes of the girls on the other teams closing in on her.

Not one, not two, not three, but every team on that track blew past Nadia as if she was a stop sign. Yet, she continued to give her all, going as fast as she could, which was much slower than when she first started. She just knew her teammates were going to whip her behind when she got off the track. So, she did what any smart person would do. She slowed down to a trot, as she was finishing up. Surely, something must have been terribly wrong with her for her to do that in a championship race. As she trotted down the final stretch, she grabbed the back of her leg and limped to the finish line. The crowd cheered her on. Falling down on the grass and rolling around in *agony*, praying her act was working, different coaches came to assist her.

Please, let the girls have some pity on me, Nadia thought, as she tried to squeeze tears from her eyes. Let's just say, she didn't get any pity at all, as they stood over her and glared down with malice in their eyes.

The thought of it all made her laugh out loud, as she got a pair of shorts and shirt from the dresser drawer and dressed. She grabbed her sneakers from the closet, which already had funky socks stuffed inside. *Who cares*, she thought since she was showering right after her workout. Her headache was easing up and a good workout was what she needed to increase her happy hormones. As she walked toward the basement, Steve wasn't in the living room. *Funny*, she thought. *Maybe he's in the bathroom in the basement.*

Heading down the basement steps, she couldn't believe her eyes. Steve was walking on the treadmill. *Why would he do that? He knows I work out every morning.*

He looked at her, adjusted the settings on the treadmill and started running.

Dressed and ready to exercise, now she couldn't, thanks to him.

"Do you know how long you might be on?" she shouted over the hum of the treadmill. "I need to walk for a few minutes, so I can get a little bit of energy to start my day."

"Nah, you should've gotten up earlier," he yelled back, adjusting the speed to run faster.

Nadia froze. She simply could not believe it.

Steve had absolutely no intention of letting her workout. Why would he hijack her time? And, he knew she was afraid to walk through the neighborhood in the morning because it's dark. Defeated, tired and worn, she walked back upstairs to take her shower.

"I hate him, I hate him, I hate him," she mumbled under her breath.

Steve's divisive tactics were too much for her. He always found ways to sabotage her happiness and take from her the simplest things.

Back when she was trying to fix healthy meals for their family, Steve would complain about his weight and she always tried to uplift him whenever she saw him looking at the tire around his belly.

"Baby, you look good to me."

"No, I don't. I'm getting fat. I really need to start eating better."

He didn't have to tell her twice. If he needed something, she made it happen for him. In fact, she was excited about doing something that would make him happy and keep him healthy.

"Well, the next time I go to the grocery store, I will buy healthier foods and we can eat better together. It will be good for the kids, too."

Steve agreed, or at least he acted as if he did.

The next day, when Nadia was on her lunch break, she checked online for healthy meals and made a grocery list.

She went to the grocery store and bought fresh vegetables, whole grains, fruits, water and one hundred percent juices. She also got olive oil, salmon, ground turkey and fresh spices. She was so excited about the change their family was making. Maybe if Steve ate better, then he would feel better about himself. Then, he might start treating her better. She knew that you felt better when you ate better and that was her way of helping their marriage along, one day at a time.

When she arrived home and started bringing in the bags of groceries, Steve was sitting on the couch with a scowl on his face. He didn't even get up to help her. As she went back out to the car to get the last of the groceries, a sinking feeling came over her. Steve made his way into the kitchen. He was going through the bags.

"Don't nobody want to eat this shit. Damn, Nadia, I'm a grown ass man. I need some food in here. Everybody ain't trying to eat like you. Why you trying to change me? What man got you wanting to eat like this?"

Every item Steve took out of the bag he threw on the floor. Was this *grown ass man* having a temper tantrum and throwing food because she wanted him to be healthy?

Tears filled her eyes, but she said nothing. She grabbed her purse and keys, left the house and drove back to the grocery store. She bought as many chips, cookies, juice, ice cream, cake desserts and any other junk that her dwindling budget could handle.

When she returned home, once again, she single-handedly carried the bags of groceries into the house. Surprisingly, Steve had cleaned up the mess he'd made. She took the groceries in the kitchen and he came in and started looking through the bags. He grabbed a snack cake and went into the living room, where he flopped his selfish ass on the couch.

"I hope you eat until you get sick, clog your arteries, overdose on sugar and grease and fucking die!" is what she wanted to say, as she walked toward the living room, but instead, she said, "Eat like you want to eat."

Since her morning routine was null and void, Nadia looked in on Danielle and Darryl. She opened their bedroom doors and looked at her babies. They were still sleeping. Their children were the best things that came out of that marriage.

It was now going on five o'clock, so she had a few extra minutes before waking them. It wasn't enough time, though, for her to grab a little more sleep, but just enough time for her to sit and think about how frustrated she was with her life.

She walked back into her bedroom and closed the door. There was a yearning in her spirit to meet with God. As if pulled by some spiritual force, she fell on her knees and then on her face. No prayer escaped her lips, but she just let her body go limp and figured that God knew the rest. What could she say that she hadn't said before? She just needed the strength to get through the day. At least it was Friday and she had the weekend to try to get it together.

The longer she stayed on her face, the heavier her body felt. She wanted to lift her head and get in the shower, but she just couldn't move herself. Uncontrollable tears flowed and mucous dripped from her nose, but she didn't care. She was a mess. She just didn't understand how she ended up here. How had her life turned into this? She cried for a few minutes more, and then suddenly, her moment was over. Her tears dried up and the heaviness was lifted. The spiritual force released her, allowing her to get up and start her day.

She made her way to the bathroom and, once again, looked in the mirror. She was a sad, broken woman. She took off her shoes and clothes and turned on the shower. No hot water. *You have got to be kidding me.* Steve must have gotten in the shower and used all the water while she was on her face seeking God. See, that was another advantage of her having that time to herself in the morning. Working out and a hot shower seemed to be all that she had and he just snatched it from her like a thief in the night. *Asshole!*

Although she just had a spiritual encounter with God, right now she just wanted to go downstairs and kick Steve's ass. She had to wash, so she jumped in the shower with the frigid water beating against her skin. *Such an asshole!* She was trembling from the cold. She had no other choice. She did a PTA—pussy, tits and armpits. Done in less than three minutes, she jumped out and grabbed her robe off the hook on the back of the door. Not only was she robbed of a nice workout, but also she was only half-clean. On the other hand, this brazen fucker had a full workout and was clean as a whistle.

She slipped her feet into her slippers and went into the kitchen to start breakfast for the kids. She took the bacon and eggs out of the refrigerator, and found the non-stick frying pan. That was the best invention ever. Opening the pack of bacon, she started placing strips in the pan when Steve sashayed into the kitchen. With a towel wrapped around his waist, he leaned against the refrigerator, staring at her.

"Why are you looking at me like that?"

"I can't believe this shit, Nadia."

"You can't believe what?"

"You can get up first thing in the morning to workout. You can come in here and fix breakfast, but you can't take care of your man?"

"Steve, I came to you last night—"

"You shouldn't have had to come to me last night," he said, rudely cutting her off. "You knew what I wanted." He smirked, looking her up and down. "But now look at you. You're in here cooking when your focus should be on me. Look, I'm outta here."

"Wait, Steve, let's talk." There was a hint of desperation in her voice.

Without looking back, Steve kept walking toward the bedroom to get dressed. He knew she was going to follow him. She always did.

She extinguished the fire from the bacon and walked into their bedroom.

Steve was sitting on the edge of the bed.

She needed to make this right or her day would be screwed. Kneeling down in front of him, she opened his towel and began massaging his shriveled dick. She hoped that they could do this quickly, make him ejaculate and then she could get back to the breakfast and get ready for work.

Looking down at her, his face held no expression.

However, her face was burning. Anger was welling up in her. Once again, this was a tactic for her to have a little peace in her home without all the sexual tension that had become a part of her daily existence.

"Stop," Steve said, moving her hands. "Get up. Things can't be on your terms. Now you wanna come in here and give me a pity blowjob just to shut me up."

"No, Steve, I felt so bad last night and I really want you now."

"Nah, maybe we can try later, but I'm just not feeling this right now."

Shit…shit…shit. Another sleepless night. She figured if he came now, then maybe he might consider leaving her alone later.

"Okay," she said. "Later."

She tightened the belt around her robe, walked back into the kitchen, washed her hands and finished making breakfast for the kids and lunch for everyone. She couldn't even think straight because she knew that, once again, sleep tonight would be out of the question.

Chapter 3

Theresa and Nadia were childhood friends. They met in elementary school and attended middle school and high school together. Although they attended different universities, they both majored in Education. They even attended the same church. Now, they worked in the same school. Sometimes, Nadia didn't know what she would do without her best friend in her life. They knew everything about each other, and were there for each other. Nadia adored her friendship with Theresa. She was her true friend, a word she never used loosely or a status she never took lightly.

As soon as Theresa walked through the doors of the school library, she knew something wasn't right with her best friend. Maybe it was kindred spirit, but she could feel when something simply wasn't intact.

"Hey, Nadia. Are you feeling okay today?"

"Yeah, I'm fine," Nadia said, not really wanting to get into what she was thinking with Theresa.

Nadia had been working in the school system for the past twelve years as an elementary school Librarian, or in modern terms, a Media Specialist. She taught library skills to students in kindergarten through fifth grade. Each class lasted for thirty minutes and her students kept her smiling. Since she was between classes, she welcomed the break when Theresa walked in.

"You sure? I looked in and saw you sitting here, staring into space."

"It's a long story, girl. We'll talk later."

"Okay, I have to go and get my class from the cafeteria. We're doing arts and crafts this afternoon, so pray for me." She chuckled. Theresa was a second grade teacher, and a great one at that.

After the doors closed behind Theresa, Nadia decided to straighten up the library shelves and put the books in order. The Dewey Decimal System can be a real pain in the ass. Looking at all of the numbers on those books can be overwhelming at times, but even today, that didn't bother her as much as the misery she had to look forward to at the end of her workday. And to top it all off, she had to give a presentation at a staff meeting right after school.

Nadia stopped shelving the books and looked around the library. When she first started at Kinnville Elementary School, the library was a complete mess. It was dingy and dark. She put her heart and soul into changing that library around and making it the nucleus of the school. Now, all meetings, parties and staff lunches were held in the area she shaped, molded and made her own.

In many ways, changing that library changed the tone of the school. It was where most teachers hung out during the day, taking a short break from their classes. The principal praised her creativity. Nadia had the custodians move the shelves to open up the space. They also re-painted the walls from the depressing grayish blue to canary yellow. She donated the old, worn, out-of-date books to the community centers and replaced them with new, exciting books that even non-readers would enjoy. That was her mission, finding a way to reach the students that didn't like to read and it started with making the library an inviting, fun place to visit.

Using her own money, Nadia purchased bright, vibrant posters and banners and had them strategically placed around the library. She ordered literary throw rugs from educational catalogs and yellow chairs. She made her work area a place she enjoyed coming to every day. The library was her baby and it was appreciated by everyone. So, she wondered, as she continued shelving, why she couldn't get that same appreciation for the things she did in her own house that never seemed to feel like a home.

Just as Nadia was about to go into Pity Party Land, her first grade class was waiting at the door. The children were so cute and didn't have a care in the world. She wondered if any of their parents experienced some of what she experienced at home.

As the students entered and took their seats, Nadia looked around and decided she was not going to read the story to them that she planned. She was just too exhausted to be that animated. A surge of guilt shot through her, but then she realized they had no clue she was going to read them a story anyway, and the guilt quickly vanished.

"Good afternoon, class." She walked toward the front of the library.

"Good afternoon, Mrs. Stevenson," the class said in unison.

Nadia took a brief second to look at the eighteen innocent faces and thought about her own first and third grade children. They had that same innocent look, too, yet unbeknownst to them, a silent war was raging at home, in their very presence.

"Today, we are going to check out books."

There was cheering from the students because this meant they could walk around with their shelf markers and choose one book they liked. There was also cheering from Nadia on the inside because she didn't have to use her brain and everyone was happy.

At the end of the thirty-minute class, each student had a book and sat at their tables quietly reading when their teacher, Ms. Kay, arrived. She gathered her students, made them push in their chairs and guided them quietly out of the library and down the hall. Ms. Kay had her children trained properly and they didn't mess with her. Teachers like that made the world a better place.

Nadia had fifteen minutes before her final class of the day. She sat down at her desk and checked her e-mail. As usual, there were numerous, pointless e-mails from various staff members. Sometimes, she wondered if people just wanted attention and tried to get it in any format. Teachers brought their students to the library once a week on a specific day and at a specific time. The schedule was set in stone at the beginning of the school year.

So why did teachers send e-mails asking if they were going to have library time on the same day, at the same time, every week? *Get a life.*

As Nadia scrolled down the list of e-mails, her heart immediately raced. Pausing for a few seconds, she took a few deep breaths before opening the message from Steve.

> *Look, Nadia, I'm tired of always having to second-guess things with you. I'm not sure how much longer I can take this. What I want from you costs you nothing, but you can't just do what I ask. You and the kids are the most important things in the world to me, but you keep pushing me away. You are always praying, but what are you praying for? What you need to be talking to God about is how to treat your man. I don't ask you for much, but what I do ask for I expect for it to be given to me. I can't pick up Darryl today so you're going to have to get him on your way home.*

Nadia's stomach dropped into her lap. She heard the library door open. It was her last first grade class for the day.

"Come on in and sit down," she said from behind her desk.

The class quietly took their seats.

Nadia hit reply.

I can't get Darryl today. I have to give a presentation after school and I was going to get Danielle and take her to the grocery store with me. Can you please get him?

Nadia looked up from her computer to see twenty, first grade students looking her in the face. Did her facial expression give off some sort of *don't-mess-with-me* message, or were they well-trained five and six year olds?

Nadia checked out books with her last class and they were just as thrilled as the previous first graders. She was on autopilot. When the teacher picked up her students and left the library, she returned to her computer to find a simple e-mail message from Steve.

No.

Sighing heavily, Nadia simply couldn't focus on Steve right then. She had to focus on her presentation that afternoon on the new library software that would allow students and teachers online access to the circulation system from their personal computers. After the final announcements and dismissal, Mr. Lowe, a fourth grade teacher and one of Nadia's good friends, came into the library.

"You ready to give your presentation?" he asked, pulling out a chair and taking a seat. Mr. Lowe was a nice looking, bald, dark-skinned man with a neatly, trimmed salt and pepper beard and mustache framing his mouth. They got along from the moment they met. She liked the way he treated people, and he was just a good-natured man that didn't seem to get sidetracked by a lot of bullshit. It was kind of funny though, watching his lean, six-foot-four-inch, frame struggling to sit in the yellow chairs clearly meant for elementary-sized children.

"I'm ready for it to be over with," she said, straightening up the papers on her circulation desk. "The school day is just about over, but I feel like my day is just beginning."

"What do you mean?"

"I don't even feel like talking about it right now."

Nadia had shared some of what she endures at home with Mr. Lowe, but of course, she couldn't tell him everything. She felt there were some things that people wouldn't understand. All Mr. Lowe knew was that her husband was a sex fiend. Although he would laugh when she would tell him bits and pieces, he really had no clue what she really went through.

"Okay, I can respect you not wanting to talk right now. Do you need any help with anything else?"

Nadia pointed toward her projector. "If it's not too much trouble, can you please start setting that up for me while I run to the ladies room?"

"Sure."

Walking out of the library, Nadia was trying to figure out how to cut her presentation short because now she had to go across town to pick up her son and daughter. She guessed going to the grocery store was out.

Frustrated, she pushed through the bathroom door. *Steve can be such an ass!*

⁓ ⁓ ⁓

Staff members were already filling up the little chairs. She had to go to a couple of training sessions and learn how to use the new technology that she was to present to the staff and now it just didn't matter. So far, every part of her day had to be adjusted because of Steve.

Right before the training, Nadia looked through her notes to see what she could change or leave out.

"Mrs. Stevenson, may I see you for a minute?"

Nadia didn't see Mr. James, the principal, walk into the library. The staff was steadily filing in, talking amongst themselves, and she was in a slight panic, looking through her notes.

"Sure."

"I know that I'm asking a bit much of you, but would it be possible for you to make this a two-day training session? Some of our staff needs a little more help with technology and I just don't think that we can give them too much in one day. I know that this is a last minute request, but as I walk around, I notice the lack of use of technology in the classrooms."

Look at God.

"It's not a problem at all. I will just cut my presentation in half and go a little slower through each step."

"You're the greatest," Mr. James said, placing his arm around her shoulder. "We can discuss a day when you can do part two of this training."

Mr. James never moved his arm, as he brought the meeting to order. His touch should have felt no different from Steve Harvey putting his arm around a Family Feud contestant, trying to win the grand prize. However, his touch was surprisingly electrifying to Nadia. Mr. James was introducing her to a staff that already knew her, and she was getting moist; her vagina throbbed over his simple touch.

Mr. James was not physically attractive to her at all. He's not ugly, just non-descript. He stood about five-feet-nine and he refused to cut off all of his hair even though he's balding. His fingers seemed to be a little thin, which made her wonder if he had a pencil dick. However, he did wear nice suits every day and walked with a little swag. Not to mention, his face would kind of light up when he smiled. But, something about his friendly touch had turned on the faucet, causing her juices to flow rapidly.

After Mr. James finished his short introduction and removed his arm, Nadia returned to her senses, her pulsating pussy died down and she was able to give one hell of a training session. For that hour, she didn't even think about what she would be facing when she walked out of that school for the weekend.

At the end of the session, Nadia answered a few questions, and then packed up and left. She needed to beat the Friday traffic, which was hell in Washington, DC. Throwing everything in the back seat of her Toyota Camry, she started the car. She really wanted to take a short nap, but she knew she had to hurry and get across town. Most people were excited about the weekend. Not Nadia. She could never be sure how her weekend would play out. She felt like she didn't have time to rest and, at that very moment, she could feel fatigue creeping up on her as she drove out of the school parking lot and merged into traffic.

Nadia decided to listen to Will Downing. She had to be extra careful though because Will's ass made her want to touch herself. His sultry voice does something to her and she needed to hear him. Unbeknownst to Will Downing, he gave her goose bumps in places she didn't know were possible. She wished her life could be as smooth as the sounds coming from Will. *I try and I try and I try and I try and you know…*

"Yeah, sing to me Willy!" Nadia blurted without a care, as she turned up the volume on the car stereo. "You know what, Will? I try, too."

She released an exhausting sigh.

Chapter 4

As traffic picked up a little, Nadia breathed a sigh of relief. Her mind wandered back to Mr. James, and why his simple gesture lit a fire in her panties. What was that all about? She had never given that man a second thought, yet earlier he caused a riot between her thighs. She tried to recreate that sexy feeling by thinking of his touch again, but it was gone. *I guess it was a momentary thing*, she thought.

Now that she wouldn't be going to the grocery store, she had to figure out what they were going to have for dinner. She really didn't want to talk to Steve, but if she brought him something home that he wanted to eat, then possibly her weekend could start on a good note.

Digging inside her satchel purse for her cell phone, she pulled it out and pressed his name on her phone, and it rang four times.

"Please, let him answer," she said out loud.

Steve had her so twisted in the mind that even the simplest things were a chore to her. If he didn't answer, she would have to try to figure out what he wanted to eat and if she made the wrong choice, then she would have to face the music.

"Yeah," he answered on the fifth ring.

"Hey, how are you doing?" she asked, trying to get a feel for the type of mood he was in.

"Nadia, what do you want?"

"Well, I'm on my way to get the kids and I wondered if you wanted any Chinese food tonight?"

Maybe she hit a happy nerve in him or something because his tone changed dramatically. "That's cool. Get me a shrimp mei fun and two egg rolls."

"Okay. If you need anything else just call me."

He hung up with no response.

Feeling somewhat relieved, she figured that maybe he would let her get a little rest, especially since she was doing him a favor by picking up their son.

Nadia pulled up to Darryl's school and parked. She was exhausted. Her son was a ball of energy and she needed a few seconds to prepare for her baby. So, she listened to the Michael Baisden Show for a few minutes. He always discussed a topic that made her think and that day's topic was Dream Killers. She couldn't listen to that right now, as she knew deep down that she was living with a dream killer and she didn't need to be reminded of it.

Inside the school, Darryl was stretched out on the floor, pushing a toy car back and forth and making motorized sounds.

Ms. Davis, the after school provider, spotted Nadia and smiled. She turned her attention to Darryl. "Your mother is here, Darryl." A beautiful, older woman around sixty, Ms. Davis had flawless, chocolate skin and it was evident by her shapely physique that she was a showstopper in her younger days.

Darryl looked up, left his car, ran to his mother, and gave her a huge hug.

"Hey, baby."

"Mommy, where's Daddy?"

"I think he had to work late, baby. Hurry and get your things."

"'Kay, Mommy."

Nadia had absolutely no idea why Steve couldn't pick up Darryl. He said nothing and she didn't ask.

Watching her handsome son run off to the coat rack to retrieve his book bag and coat, he looked like a miniature Steve with pieces of her sprinkled here and there. He would quickly grow into an extremely handsome, young man, a soon-to-be lady-killer.

"Mrs. Stevenson, I need to talk to you about Darryl's payments," said Ms. Davis, with concern on her face.

"I'm sorry, Ms. Davis. What do you mean?"

"Well, did you know that you are behind on one payment and Darryl's next payment is due today?"

Nadia looked at Ms. Davis like she was crazy. "I don't understand. My husband pays for this every two weeks. If this is behind, then why weren't we notified before today?"

"I'm sorry for the misunderstanding, Mrs. Stevenson. I did tell Mr. Stevenson and he told me that you would take care of everything when you came to pick up Darryl today."

Nadia felt like a damn fool and Ms. Davis looked like she was embarrassed for her. Knowing it showed on her face, she didn't want to alarm Ms. Davis or give her any negative impressions about how her home life was fucked up.

"You know what? Now that I think about it, Steve did mention that to me," she lied.

Ms. Davis didn't believe her, as it clearly showed on her turned-up face.

Feeling uneasy and beyond embarrassed, Nadia fidgeted a bit. "I've been so busy that it must've slipped my mind. How much is it? I can write you a check."

Looking through her purse for the checkbook was easier than looking Ms. Davis in the eye.

"I'm sorry, Mrs. Stevenson. It's in the contract that we do not accept checks if a payment is more than two weeks late. We can take a money order or a cashier's check in the full amount of five hundred ten dollars." Nadia could've fainted on the spot. "It's two hundred forty for both sessions and a thirty dollar late fee."

Nadia was heated and the tension building inside of her was plastered on her face. She couldn't go to the grocery store if she wanted to. Now what the hell was she going to do? Her bank was on the other side of town. She looked at Darryl who was bundled up and sweating.

"Take off your coat for a few seconds, lil' man. I have to run across the street for a minute."

"Good because I'm hot, Mommy." Darryl struggled with the zipper. Nadia helped him with his coat and kissed him on the cheek. He ran back to the car that he left on the floor and started making those same car noises. Just like that, he was in his own world.

"Ms. Davis, I will be right back. I'm going to get the money order." Nadia walked toward the door.

Fighting back tears, and racing across the street to the liquor store, she had just over six hundred dollars in her account and now it was gone. When she and Steve decided to split up the bills, she thought things would get better financially for them, but that was a huge error in judgment on her part. When she has her emotional spending rants, it's with *her* money. She never touched *his* money.

When Steve and Nadia first married, they decided to put everything in one account. That was a mistake because both of them had ATM cards to the account. Too many times, their bank statements reflected fifty dollars missing here, one hundred dollars missing there, but what she did notice was that he never used his ATM card in any stores unless it was the gas station. He always withdrew cash from the bank teller. Whenever she asked Steve about the number of times he went to the ATM machine in a month, his response was always the same.

"I'm a grown ass man and I'm gonna have money in my pocket."

Nadia certainly understood that if he worked he should be able to have some ends. So, she tried another approach.

They sat down, put all the bills on the table and pilfered through them until they came to an agreement. Every payday Friday, Steve would get one hundred fifty dollars from his paycheck, which did not include gas or groceries. That worked because their paydays were the same. That would be his play around money. Nadia would get seventy-five dollars per paycheck to play around with on the same terms.

By Sunday, money would be missing from her purse. When asked, he would laugh and say that he spent his money and he needed to get through the week. She had no clue how Steve blew through one hundred fifty dollars in two days, but his spending problem became her problem. She had to figure out how to keep money in his pocket until next payday and make him happy, even though he didn't own up to his end of the bargain. She wouldn't even get an opportunity to spend her seventy-five dollars because she would end up giving it to him once he ran through his money. Steve would nickel and dime her little money until it was gone and then have a complete bitch-fit about being broke.

This vicious cycle was just another form of stress Nadia endured damn near daily. She didn't really want to rock the boat because as long as Steve had a little bit of money in his pocket, he seemed, at least for a hot minute, to be content. Then she would get pieces of peace. But, it was tough just watching the money going down the drain and she had nothing to show for it.

Finally, enough was enough. Again, she wrote out all the bills and gave Steve a few to pay from his check, one of them being Darryl's daycare. She would pay the rest. That took some of the strain off of her from trying to figure everything out and it put some responsibility on him. She suggested that they put their money in separate accounts and, surprisingly, he was thrilled with that idea. That way, no matter what, he could do what he wanted with his money and he could no longer touch or control hers.

That was until now.

She walked inside the crowded liquor store and looked at the vast variety of spirits. She didn't drink, but she wondered if maybe she should start. She guessed people were getting ready for the weekend. She went to the ATM machine at the back of the store and withdrew the money. Then, she went to the counter to get the money order. She had to pay a three-dollar ATM fee and two dollars for a money order. Now, she was counting every dollar. She thanked the cashier for the money order and walked out of the store. Her head started throbbing.

One, two, three…Nadia, you're going to be all right, she said to herself.

She raced across the street to the daycare, filled out the money order and handed it to Ms. Davis, who already had Darryl in his coat and ready to go.

Again, Ms. Davis gave Nadia a sorrowful look, as she gathered her son and went to the car.

Chapter 5

"Mommy, is God everywhere?"

"Yes."

"Is He in the car?"

"Yes."

"Where?"

"We can't see God."

"Why?"

Darryl was on a roll. He was staring out the window and everything he wanted to ask about, he did.

"Because God is a spirit and He dwells within us."

"What does 'dwells' mean?"

"Lives."

"God lives in me?"

"Yes."

"Why?"

Nadia had to do something quick. Her saving grace was that she was almost at her daughter's school who would become his next victim. As she pulled up to the school, she remembered the Chinese food. *More money coming out of my pocket.* Before she got out of the car to get Danielle, she ordered the food from her cell phone.

Darryl and Nadia walked in the school to her daughter's class. Danielle was sitting at the table doing her homework. Nadia's headache seemed to be getting worse.

Danielle was a beautiful little girl. Knowing people always thought their daughter was gorgeous, she had the right to think that, as her daughter really was gorgeous. She has eyes that seemed to glisten and when she smiled, her face lit up. What she loved about her most though was that at the tender age of eight, she already understood responsibility and she made very mature choices. For instance, she would finish her homework on Friday, so she wouldn't have to worry about it on the weekend. She just loved that girl.

Danielle looked up at Nadia and smiled. "Hi, Mommy."

"Hi, baby. Come on let's go."

Darryl ran over to the bookshelf.

"Mommy, you okay?" Danielle asked.

Danielle knew when her mother was upset. When Nadia was pregnant with Danielle, if she got upset or worried, Danielle would ball up tightly on the right side of her stomach. Nadia would rub that area and pray until Danielle came out of that ball, which was painful for Nadia. Whatever it was that was bothering her, Nadia had to let it go. She didn't want to put that tension on her unborn child.

"I'm fine, baby," she said, giving her a kiss on her cheek.

Danielle packed her book bag and put on her coat. "I'm ready, Mommy."

"Come on, Darryl" Nadia called out.

Darryl closed the book he was reading, put it on the shelf and ran to open the door for his mother and sister, which was one thing she really loved about her son. As long as he was around, Danielle and she never had to open a door. He loved doing that for them and they would let him do it.

As soon as they got settled in the car, Darryl started in on Danielle.

"Danny, did you know that God lives in me?"

"Yes," Danielle answered, fully aware of what was coming.

Nadia breathed a small sigh of relief and let Darryl hammer away at his big sister.

"Does God live in you, too?"

"Yes, Darryl, now leave me alone," said an irritated Danielle.

"God is da bomb dot com!" exclaimed an excited Darryl.

The questioning and fussing continued between her children as they arrived at the Chinese restaurant. The three of them hurried inside and went to the counter.

"Mommy, I can't wait to get home and eat," Danielle said, licking her lips.

"I'm gonna eat all of your food," taunted Darryl.

"No you're not!" Danielle shouted.

"If both of y'all don't shut up, nobody's eating anything," Nadia said with a slightly raised voice. "Try me and see."

Danielle and Darryl shut up immediately.

Nadia went to the counter and paid thirty-three dollars for the food. She wanted to cry. *I am completely broke and tired as hell.*

They got back in the car and headed home.

I hate him, I hate him, I hate him, she thought.

∾ ∾ ∾

Pulling up to the house, Nadia's heart picked up its pace. What was she nervous about? He's the one who screwed her. She grabbed the food and Danielle and Darryl grabbed their things and got out the car. As she inserted her key into the lock, she was secretly wishing she had a place just for her and her children. She opened the door and Steve was lying on the couch, watching ESPN.

This bastard is just sitting here chilling out while I'm running around town depleting my fucking bank account, she thought, closing the door behind her.

"Hey, lady," Steve said with a wide smile on his face. He looked like a male version of Danielle.

"Hey," she said half-heartedly. "Danny and Darryl, go put your things up, wash your hands and get ready to eat."

The kids headed to the back of the house and she went into the kitchen with the food, with Steve following on her heels like a lost puppy dog.

"Mmmm, smells good," Steve said, looking into the bag.

His demeanor seemed to be very pleasant, which put her at a crossroad. Does she mention the money for the daycare or enjoy the pleasantries coming from her husband? She chose the pleasantries, pushing everything in her day to some area of her mind and put it on layaway.

"I'll fix the plates," he said. "You check on the kids."

Nadia went into the living room and sat on the couch for a few minutes. She closed her eyes and listened to the kids arguing about whether or not the Disney Channel was better than Nickelodeon.

"Come on and eat," Steve said, just as she was really starting to relax.

She struggled to get up, but she did make it to the dining room table. Danielle said grace and everyone dug in.

Steve and the kids joked around and he even joined in on the Disney-Nickelodeon argument, giving reasons as to why they were both the best. Nadia just listened.

After she ate, fatigue started hitting her with full force. "Look, everybody, I'm exhausted. I'm going to go in the room and lay down for a few minutes."

"Okay, Mommy," Danielle and Darryl said in unison.

"Yeah, baby, you go ahead. I'll be in to give you a massage a little later. You look beat."

Oh really? She got up from the table, wondering what brought about that change.

Nadia walked into her room and lay across the bed. She sensed that Steve was fully aware of what he had done to her and this was his way of making up. Nadia always thought men weren't very good at expressing themselves and that they showed how they felt through actions. She wasn't sure if this was right or wrong, but the theory was going to hold true in her mind for now.

Nadia closed her eyes and thought back over her day. From the time she woke up until now, her emotions have been out of whack. How she managed to get through all of this she would never know. From Steve being on the treadmill because she didn't have the energy to have sex with him, to her having to pick up Darryl to losing all her money and everything in between, she was drained. Every time she thought about her money, a sinking feeling would hit her. Now that she was getting a massage from her husband, she tried desperately to deny how she was feeling.

Nadia, Steve is trying to show you how much he cares for you, she said to herself. Although she tried convincing herself, she knew the truth.

Nadia didn't know when she finally fell asleep, but she was awakened by Steve pulling off her pants.

"What are you doing?" she asked groggily.

"I'm going to give my baby a massage. You deserve it."

Steve was smiling at her and she got a glimpse of the man she fell in love with years ago. After Steve pulled off her pants, he slipped off her panties.

"Sit up, Na Na."

Steve hadn't called her Na Na in years. Was she wrong about her husband? Had she jumped to conclusions about things that she didn't understand?

Nadia sat up and Steve slowly lifted her shirt over her head and tossed it to the side.

"I want you to lay on your stomach for me."

"Wait a minute. What about the kids?"

"They've been sleep for about two hours now."

Nadia looked at the clock. It was one-thirteen in the morning. She had no idea that she'd slept that long.

Steve went to the bathroom and got the baby oil and a towel. She got up so that he could place the towel under her. Then she lay on her stomach on top of the towel.

"Lay down this way baby," Steve said, motioning for her to lay with her head at the foot of the bed. That was different, but she didn't care. It was a nice ending to a rough day, and all the tension and hurt was released. For once, Steve was right. She did deserve this.

"This is for you, Na Na. Close your eyes and enjoy."

He walked over to the CD player and put on one of her favorite songs by Will Downing, *For All We Know*. Will's voice filled the room. Steve knew how she felt about that man. He didn't touch her at all while the song played. She was able to relax. Never wanting to let go of that feeling, everything about that moment felt good. Almost too good to be true.

When the song ended, Steve let the CD continue to play. She could sense him making his way over to her. Before she knew it, baby oil was dripping on the back of her legs. He gently rubbed the oil into her skin and massaged her leg muscles. He made his way down to her feet and took his time massaging each foot. He pulled her toes and then worked his way back up her legs. This was the best feeling ever. He was so gentle with her, yet the massage was firm enough. As he made his way to her butt—or her dunk as he called it—he pushed, massaged, rolled and rubbed in all the right places. Steve slid his hands up her body and massaged her back.

It was heaven. She slightly opened her eyes and saw that he was butt naked. Maybe he undressed when her eyes were closed as she listened to Will Downing. Steve positioned himself in front of her and moved his hands from the nape of her neck down to her back, as his rock hard penis stroked across her face. As he massaged his way back up to her neck, he took his penis in his hand and pressed it against her lips. He began to pry her lips open and the wetness from the head of his penis gliding across her mouth felt like lip-gloss.

Nadia moved her head back, not wanting to suck no damn dick. She wanted her massage. Steve firmly pushed her head back down and tried to force his penis inside her mouth.

Should I say something? She had to say something. She kept her lips pursed and jerked her head back. He grabbed the head of his penis and actually tried to pry her lips apart. She shook her head violently, rolled over and sat up.

"Steve, what are you doing? I thought you were giving *me* a massage."

"Damn, Nadia, you're always ruining the moment."

I guess I'm not Na Na anymore. The moment was ruined.

Steve looked angry and backed away.

"Wait a minute. I was just asking because I was confused. I...I just thought you were giving me a massage, that's all."

"Fuck it, Nadia. You're always fucking shit up. I let you get some sleep, put the kids to sleep and try to pamper you and this is how you treat me?"

Steve pushed her to the side, snatched the towel from under her, and wrapped the towel around his waist and walked out the bedroom.

"What in the hell just happened?" she asked aloud.

Nadia couldn't even cry. She thought of going after him, but she didn't know what to say. What could she do differently this time that she hadn't already done to make things right before? He tried and she blew it.

Now she was laying there butt naked, wide-awake and anxious as hell, wondering what tomorrow would hold.

Chapter 6

For the umpteenth time, Nadia suffered through the night in an uneasy sleep because she was beating her own ass. Why couldn't she just let things go? If she had simply done what he wanted, maybe she would have been able to sleep. She felt guilty as hell because she felt she had let Steve down. Yes, they were having problems, but how was she helping the situation if she didn't let him spoil her and show her that he was sorry?

However, Nadia still had a hard time letting go of the daycare fiasco. She was so confused.

As daylight broke, she heard Steve moving around in the room. She pretended to be sleeping, hoping he would just go away.

Her prayers were answered.

Steve tapped her on the shoulder. He was dressed in his basketball gear and shoes, with a sports bag draped over his shoulder.

"Look, I'm going out to play ball with the fellas," he said, walking out of the bedroom.

Moments later, the front door closed. She didn't move until she heard the engine of his car and then she knew he was gone. He wasn't in the house. He wasn't near her. He was away from her.

"That motherfucker is gone!" she sang out, but not loud enough to wake Darryl and Danielle.

With renewed energy, she jumped up and danced on the bed. She wasn't going to be bothered about sex this morning. And, to top it all off, her period was coming tomorrow. Yes! Monthly Mary came every twenty-six days like clockwork. Although she was starting to cramp, she was getting a break from sex. An extended break. It's crazy when you can have two kids in the house and it feels like a mini vacation when your husband is gone. It's even crazier to know you have a killer menstrual cycle and you look forward to that rather than having sex with your husband.

It was only seven-thirty-five in the morning. She decided to call her parents because they were always up at the crack of dawn. Her father answered the phone quite chipper, sounding like he had been up for hours.

"Hey, baby, I was just thinking about you."

"Hey, Daddy. What are y'all doing?"

"Nothing much. Your mama is over here getting on my nerves." He chuckled.

Nadia's parents have been together for forty-one years and both were retired. Forty-one years. That's a long, damn time. She thought she knew the secret to their marriage. The majority of her childhood, her mother worked during the day for the Federal government, and her father worked at night as a bus driver for Metro. Any marriage on Earth should be able to survive that kind of work schedule. The only real time they spent together was on weekends, and that was spent either at track meets, basketball games or any extracurricular activities her sister and she were involved in. Her mother would also take them to theatrical plays or movies, and her father was always good for the let's-go-get-ice-cream run.

Talk about an ideal situation. Her parents probably jumped all over each other when they got the chance because they had an opportunity to miss each other. Unlike her situation.

Sometimes she wished that motherfucker would leave and never come back and that's what she wanted to happen today. However, she knew that was nothing but wishful thinking, as his ass had no place else to go.

"Well, Daddy, I didn't want anything. I was just calling y'all this morning."

"Where are my grandbabies?"

"They're still sleeping."

"I want to see my grandbabies. If you feel like bringing them here, they can stay over tonight. Maybe then your mama will leave me alone."

Nadia laughed. *Lord, what did I do to deserve all of this today?* First, the human energizer left out to go play basketball and now her kids will be gone.

"I sure do feel like bringing them," she said.

"Don't worry about bathing or feeding them. Just wake them up and bring them. You already know we have clothes here and I'll fix them some breakfast."

"Daddy, I don't mean to disrespect you, but I gotta get off of this phone. You're holding me up from getting these rug rats to you." She chuckled.

"Well hurry on up then," he said, and then hung up.

Nadia's father always had to have the last word before he hung up the phone. She swore if she got the last word in on him he would call her back just to talk, get the last word and then hang up on her.

"Get up," she yelled. "Get up, get up, get up!"

Awakened from a peaceful slumber, Danielle and Darryl walked out of their rooms, rubbing their eyes with confusion.

"Mommy, why are you yelling?" Danielle asked, still wiping her eyes, wearing canary yellow pajamas with hearts plastered all over them. Her hair was all over her head. She looked so cute.

"Because she's our mom and she can yell at us," Darryl said, standing beside her donning Spiderman pajamas.

"She's not gonna let you drink any Kool-Aid this morning, so you can just stop kissing up," Danielle snapped.

"I don't want Kool-Aid." Darryl looked at Danielle, as if he wanted to punch her in the stomach.

"Listen, you two don't have time to argue and no one is getting any Kool-Aid this early in the morning. You have three minutes to put on your shoes and your jackets,"

"Where are we going?" Danielle asked.

"Over Grandma and Granddaddy's house."

"Yayyy!" they said in unison, jumping for joy.

Nadia's offspring ran into their rooms to get dressed and Nadia went into her bathroom, washed her face and brushed her teeth and, from her closet, chose something quick to wear. She threw on gray sweats, a gray jacket that didn't go with her sweats, shoes and a baseball cap. When she walked into the living room, the kids donned their hats and coats, waiting patiently.

"Y'all were quick," Nadia acknowledged. "Let's go."

Enclosed in a car with two kids with morning breath was probably a bad idea. Her car smelled like day-old greens. The blessing was when her parents kept the kids; she never needed to pack anything because they had a room and all the necessities in place for them.

"I'm hungry," Darryl whined.

"Son, please stop talking." Nadia held her nose and laughed.

"I'm hungry, too," Danielle chimed in.

Nadia frowned. "Oh…umm…you can just be quiet, too."

When they realized she was playing with them about their breath, her silly children did the unthinkable. They opened their little, funky mouths and started breathing as hard as they could. They were laughing so hard, their eyes glistened with tears. Tears were filling her eyes, too, but not from laughter. Their breath from the Chinese food from the night before was strong enough to make her eyes water.

They rode to her parents' house playing the Funky Breath game. As they pulled up to the thirty-five-year-old, four-story, brick house, she reminisced how she lived in that house all her life until she left for college. She always wanted her own family and a husband that adored her. Never in a million years did she think she would be unhappy coming home damn near every day. She wondered if anyone else she knew that was married felt the same way.

Nadia's father was standing on the porch, waiting for them. Although the kids' breath was lethal, she told them to give her a kiss on the cheek before they got out of the car. Danielle leaned in from the back seat, kissed her and got out of the car.

"I love you, Mommy," she said and closed the door.

"I love you, too, Mommy," Darryl said, leaning in and kissing her on the cheek. He opened the back door, leaned over to her very quickly, licked the side of her face, jumped out of the car and closed the door.

Nadia rubbed the side of her face. "Ugh!"

Darryl was laughing uncontrollably.

Her father walked over to the car and gave her a kiss on the cheek. "Now go somewhere and leave us alone." He chuckled.

"You don't have to worry about me bothering you, that's for sure." She smiled.

Nadia watched as her father walked toward his front door, with Danielle and Darryl on his heels.

Time to myself, she thought, as she backed out of the driveway and headed home.

Nadia felt free. So many thoughts permeated her mind about what she could do with her time. She put a Michael Franks CD into the CD changer and let his cool, smooth sound help her to decide. *"I'd rather be happy than right,"* she crooned along with

Michael. "I'm with you on that one brother," she said, as she hit Interstate 495 heading back home.

Twenty minutes later, Nadia walked inside her house and sat on the couch. It wasn't even nine o'clock yet. Her cell phone rang. It was Theresa.

"Hey girl," she answered.

"You sound wide awake," Theresa said.

"I am. The kids are gone. The ass is gone. And, now I'm trying to figure out what to do with my day."

Theresa laughed. "Well, you want to go and hang out at the mall, maybe grab a little something to eat and chill?"

Nadia thought about Theresa's suggestion. She couldn't remember the last time she just chilled out and did something for her. It sounded like fun. Besides, she wanted to be out of the house when Steve returned.

"Yeah, we can do that. Let me get a little workout on to get my day started and get ready and then I will come over to your house."

"Cool. Maybe I will walk or do some sort of exercise, too."

"I'll call you when I'm on my way."

"See you then, big head."

"Yo mama," she retorted and hung up.

Smiling, Nadia tossed her cell phone on the couch and went into her room to change into a tank top and shorts. She stopped and looked at herself in the mirror. She was in good shape for a forty-year-old woman, and she wasn't bad looking either. She wasn't' beauty pageant material, but she could hold her own. A dark-skinned sister with a measurement of 34-29-41, it was obvious everything she ate went straight to her big ol' booty and thighs. Admiring her firm bottom, she smiled at Theresa's words: "Your ass is your money maker, girl."

Nadia then looked at her hair. She loved her chic, bobbed style with golden streaks. She remembered when she first got the cut; complete strangers complimented her on the style and the color. But, when she walked in the house and Steve looked at her, he didn't say two words. She knew, at that moment, that she must've looked damn good. She didn't say anything, but she definitely has hater radar. She just knew there were times when she had to be smart enough to act like she didn't know what was going on. So, from his non-response, she knew she was going to rock that cut. It was the one thing she felt she could control.

Nadia went down into the basement and did a nice, thirty-minute aerobic walk with on the treadmill with two-pound weights. As she was walking, she thought about the other morning when Steve stopped her workout. *Asshole.*

Staying curvy was her mission and adding a little weight to her walk was the simple trick. She saw advertisements for workouts that had people jumping, punching and moving around like mad. She tried a few of those, but got discouraged because she didn't have that kind of time or energy every day. The best thing for her was to get moving daily. Anything will work if you just stick to it. In the same respect, nothing will work if you don't. Therefore, she settled for walking every day for thirty minutes with two-pound weights, working her arms as she pleased and contracting her abdominal muscles simultaneously. And, it worked.

Nadia finished her walk, did three sets of ten squats, four real push-ups, and then stretched out. Sweat poured off her, but she felt so good. *I need more time like this to myself*, she thought, as she walked upstairs to get cleaned up.

Nadia wrapped her hair and jumped in the shower. Warm water was the love of her life. She put on exfoliating gloves, lathered them with soap and exfoliated her entire body. She put the baby oil on while she was still in the shower and then she got out. Her skin felt amazing afterwards and she let her body air dry as she washed her face and brushed her teeth at the sink.

Nadia stepped out the bathroom and, once again, looked at her nakedness in the full-length mirror. She was feeling sexy as hell. Was it the workout mixed with the dead skin removal shower? Or, was it that she was finally alone and had a chance to get to know herself? She wanted to hold onto that feeling forever. Men and women often complimented her, yet she felt like a tired, old woman most of the time. However, this morning she felt alive and ready to go. Until her cell phone rang.

"Hello."

It was Steve. "What are you and the kids doing?"

Nervous energy shot through her. She sat on the edge of the bed and rested her head in her hand. Where did that sexy feeling go?

"I took the kids to Ma and Daddy's house."

"What?"

"Daddy said that he wanted to see his kids today, so I took them over there." She felt like a child about to be chastised.

Steve was fully aware that she always talked to her parents early in the morning, but she could just feel his selective amnesia was about to kick in, and he was getting ready to act like she had committed a crime.

"I said they're with their grandparents."

There was an uncomfortable pause.

"So, what are you getting ready to do since you didn't let me know you wouldn't have the kids?" His tone was accusatory. What difference did it make? He wasn't there.

"I'm getting dressed to go out with Theresa for a little while. We're just going to the mall and to get something to eat. We won't be gone long." She tried to downplay her day.

"Well, I might be going out with the fellas tonight."

Nadia wanted to jump up and out of her skin and start doing the Wobble dance. Her day just couldn't have gotten any better.

"Okay, well y'all have fun." She tried not to sound too excited.

"I might come back later or I might just buy something to wear if I decide to chill at Malik's place." Malik was Steve's best friend of thirty years.

"Well, I know your monkey ass has the money because you damn sure didn't pay for the daycare," was what she wanted to say, but instead she prayed for the torturous call to end quickly before she had a natural fit.

"I will call you later," Steve snapped and hung up. He didn't give her a chance to say good-bye and she didn't care. He was gone! *Thank God!*

Nadia rolled across the bed and kicked her feet with excitement like a child on Christmas morning. Then she got up and Wobbled up and down the hallway until she figured she should put on some clothes and get the hell out of the house.

Chapter 7

It was a beautiful fall day. Theresa and Nadia pulled into the shopping center, and Nadia found a space and parked.

"Look, bitch," Theresa snapped. "If you want me to lose weight, then just say so! Do we have to walk a damn mile to the mall? Look at all of those spaces up front."

Theresa was right. There were plenty of spaces near the entrance, and Nadia pulled into the first one she saw…in the last row of the parking lot. She was used to walking; it didn't bother her. Besides, she despised riding around in circles just to find a closer spot. The way she saw it, the time it took to drive around looking for a closer parking space, could be spent in the mall, perusing the sales racks.

Nadia looked at Theresa with a smirk. "Lose weight?" Nadia chuckled, and turned off the engine.

They both laughed and climbed out the car.

Nadia was truly feeling herself today, as her gray BCBG sweat suit was fitting a little too snug. To be honest, everything she wore fit snug, which could be due to how she was shaped. Her clothes either hugged or hung. She chose hugged, which was what attracted Steve to her in the first place.

Steve and Nadia met while she was home on summer vacation from North Carolina Central University, which was where she learned about life. After attending Catholic school from kindergarten through high school, roaming the campus of a black university was a life changer for her.

While home on summer vacation, Nadia worked as a hostess at Bumbel's restaurant in Washington, DC. Steve was a waiter, and a good-looking, clean-cut man, with a smooth, caramel complexion and the type of eyes women would die for—deeply set. Steve was slightly taller than she was, and in great physical shape. They had hit it off instantly.

They dated through the summer and stayed together when she decided to return to North Carolina to work on her master's degree. After graduation, she moved back home and into Steve's apartment. They married one year later and her life has been nothing but a fuck fest.

Nadia wasn't clueless, as she saw signs early on. When she didn't feel like having sex, he would get an attitude. That was when she realized she'd made the mistake of compromising too early. She should've told that fool to beat it, literally, but she wanted things to remain cool, so she gave him what he wanted every time he wanted it.

Receiving a proposal should have been a happy moment, but for Nadia, it all boiled down to it being that time in her life to settle down. Hell, after receiving a Bachelor of Arts in History and a Master's of Library Science, she found a nice job as an elementary school Librarian, so all she needed was to marry and have children. Although she recognized people weren't perfect and Steve was no exception, the sex thing was something small and she chose to live with it. However, she had no idea of how small things magnified immediately after *I do*. And, Steve still worked at Bumbel's as a manager.

Reality slapped the hell out of Nadia when she and Theresa walked into Macy's. She had no money. Her face must have given way to her frustration.

"What's wrong?" Theresa asked, picking up a black, sheer blouse and holding it up to her body.

"Girl, I just want to have a nice time."

"Look, we haven't talked in a while. Let's head to the food court before we do anything else, grab a bite and let it all hang out."

"Let's go."

Nadia was amazed at all the Christmas decorations in October, which seemed too early for her, but they were truly a beautiful sight, and the mood was ripe for shopping. Vibrant sales signs were everywhere, enticing emotional shoppers such as herself to come on in, spend now and cry later.

Nadia watched as a nice-looking gentleman damn near broke his neck looking at Theresa, who stood about five-feet-six inches tall with breasts that had to be double D's, a butt to match and no stomach. She looked like a smaller version of Sandra from the television show, *227*. She chuckled, as Theresa appeared oblivious to the attention she was receiving, or maybe she was used to it. That guy was fine, and Nadia couldn't help herself, as she gawked at him when he walked by them. He was still staring. He shook his head as if to say, "Lawd have mercy," but he kept walking.

"Theresa, did you see that dude checking you out?"

"What dude?"

Nope, she didn't see him.

"Never mind." Nadia figured that same scenario would probably happen again at least a dozen more times before the day was over.

They reached the food court and decided on grilled chicken salads. Nadia and Theresa had a personal thing with eating healthy, especially after they worked out. Why put in the time and energy to exercise if you're going to mess it up all within a matter of minutes with what you eat?

"I'll pay for your food," Theresa offered. "You go find the table."

Thank God for small blessings and great friends because coming out of her pocket at all until next Friday was going to kill Nadia.

They sat down, blessed their food and then Nadia told Theresa about what happened with the daycare situation.

"You know," Theresa said between bites, "you should say something to Steve about what he did. How will he know that he did anything wrong if you don't tell him?"

"Theresa, he's a grown ass man. He knew exactly what he did."

"And you're a grown ass woman who should speak up. What are you scared of, Nadia?"

This was one of the reasons why she didn't like talking to people, even her closest friends. It was either black or white with them. The complicated stuff was in the gray area. Nadia learned years ago never to tell people what she was going through unless she made a decision about what she was going to do. The same people she vented to would hold onto what she told them forever and all she really wanted to do was release her frustrations.

"I'm not scared." She lied. She was terrified, but she wasn't exactly sure why. Steve had only been physical with her once when they got into a heated argument about his brother, Eddie, who used Steve's name and social security number when the police pulled him over for drinking and driving. Steve acted as if it wasn't a big deal and said he would handle it later.

"What the fuck you mean 'handle it later'?" she screamed at him. "You jump on me for bullshit and—" The wind was knocked out of her.

Feeling a vicious shock to her side, she went down and curled into a fetal ball. Steve had hit her with a kidney shot. As she curled up in too much pain to cry, he knelt down beside her.

"I'm sorry, baby, I'm so sorry. I didn't mean to hit you."

Steve sat beside her on the floor, pulled her up, put her head against his chest and rocked her until she fell asleep. The next morning when she woke up, he'd brought her breakfast in bed along with a long-stemmed, fresh, red rose and a tear-jerking card.

Nadia never spoke of the incident again.

Steve had to go to court and prove that it was not him, but his brother. Thankfully, it cost him nothing but another notch of hate in Nadia's gut for him.

"It's just that it's so hard sometimes," she said, stabbing her fork in the salad. Nadia was ready to switch gears from talking about her financial woes to her sexual woes, when a gentleman took a seat at the small table right next to theirs.

"Hello. Do you ladies mind if I sit here?" Mr. Sexy Ass looked directly at Nadia.

"No, help yourself," Theresa said.

Nadia didn't usually get overwhelmed by looking at men, but this thang was the sho nuff, sho nuff!

She was elated a good-looking man sat there. Before long, the three of them were engaged in a humorous discussion about how crazy people can get around the holiday season. She was very much physically attracted to him. As they laughed and joked, Nadia's mind wandered to how long Mr. Sexy Ass's stroke was. Something about this man just had big dick written all over him.

They finished eating around the same time. Theresa grabbed her and Nadia's trash to throw it away. When she walked away, Mr. Sexy Ass smiled at Nadia.

"You're a very beautiful woman."

Drip, drip, drip came from the faucet of Nadia's juices.

"Thank you," Nadia said shyly.

"Do you think we could pick up this conversation a little later on or maybe on another day?"

"I would love to, but I'm married."

"So am I." He had to admit it since he damn sure wasn't wearing a wedding ring.

"Now you know you're wrong for that," she joked, casting her eyes at his left hand.

"Hey, if we both have something to lose then we'll be extra careful," he said, looking a little more serious.

Theresa returned at that moment.

"Look," he said. "Take my card and think about it."

Nadia took the card and, instead of tearing it up as she would usually do, she put it in her purse.

"Nice meeting you," Theresa said.

"Have a great day, ladies."

Oh my muthafuckin' goodness. This man is bow-legged as hell and he has serious swag, Nadia thought, as she watched him dump his tray.

"Good looking piece of man," said Theresa.

"You ain't never lied." They laughed and high-fived. "He gave me his card and told me to call him."

"Look, Nadia, I know that you're having problems, but don't add to them."

"I won't," she said, but she wasn't so sure. At that moment, her thoughts scared her and excited her at the same time. *What if I did have an affair? How bad could it really be? He didn't want to mess up his home, so that meant he wouldn't interfere with mine. I could finally have something other than my children that would make me smile. I might actually enjoy the sex.*

Seeming to read her thoughts, Theresa advised, "Leave it be. Now let's go sample some expensive perfume."

For most of the day, they window-shopped, didn't buy a thing, and tried on clothes, shoes, and they smelled like a mixture of every perfume in the mall. Yet, this strange man kept crossing her mind. As her thoughts were getting good about him, her cell phone vibrated inside her purse. She dug deep for it, and flipped it open.

"Hello," she answered.

"Where you at?"

"Theresa and I are at the mall."

"I'm gonna go ahead and chill at Malik's until we go out later. Buy me something."

"I don't have any money."

"Figures," Steve said and hung up.

I hate him, I hate him, I hate him. I swear, if Mr. Sexy Ass walked by me right now I would do him in one of these dressing rooms in this Macy's!

They left the mall around five o'clock. Although Nadia didn't want to cut their day short, it's rare that she had an opportunity to be at home alone. Theresa was cool with leaving anyway. She had a "friend" she refused to call her man, and he wanted to take her to a seven o'clock movie.

What in the hell was going on with her? Theresa was going on and on about if she should spend a certain amount of money on a new flat screen television. "I could just wait a few more weeks until they go on sale, blah, blah, blah," she babbled.

"Uh huh," was all Nadia was able to say. Mr. Sexy Ass was all in her brain.

Nadia dropped off Theresa and headed home. She'd thought about calling her children, but changed her mind. They were fine with their grandparents, so she was excited to enjoy her time alone.

⮑ ⮑ ⮑

Nadia walked into her bedroom, feeling inspired to write. Writing was another escape for her. She would express herself through her poetry and right now, she had to do something with what she was feeling.

Grabbing her notebook from her secret place at the top of the closet, she tossed it on the bed and started undressing. Propping up on the pillows, she felt so relaxed and ready to explore her emotions. She opened the notebook to a blank page and started to flow.

Yes, I would turn into your pillow
There are places where only one man can go
You see, he meets me there after a long day
I'm ready for loving with no delay
His kisses so sweet, yes they suck me in
My head's in the pillow and we're skin to skin
His mouth makes it down into my soft place
As the back of my head rests in the pillowcase
I moan with pleasure and he likes the taste
His invasion of my space puts a grin on my face
If I jerk any harder, I will need a neck brace
He turns me over and penetrates me

Damn, I love you, Mr. Sexy
We both grab the pillow and bite on the corner
He says, "Say my name," on command I say, "Yes sir"
A pillow understands its use is infinite
You can bite it, grind on it, a pillow's the shit
It's a soft place to rest
Or make a wet, sexy mess
You better believe it when you leave it
A pillow relieves all of your stress

Now that she was officially turned on, a relaxing soak was the next step, especially since her period would be arriving soon. She tucked her notebook away in the closet. Giggling as she got her daughter's Mr. Bubble hypoallergenic bubble bath, and as much as she loved scented lotions and such, she just couldn't use those things in the tub. *Can you say yeast city?* That Mr. Bubble is great; bubbles for days. She turned on the television to the Smooth Groove channel, lit two candles in the bathroom and ran the water, making the bubbly water as hot as she could stand it, and climbed in. That warm water was just the invitation she needed, as she slid down in the sudsy water, emerged to her neck.

Simply relaxing, she closed her eyes and thought of that fine ass man that captured her mind from the moment he said, "Hello." The thought of his lips and his sexy ass eyes caused her hands to roam. Immersed in a fantasyland of her own, she massaged her breasts, as she imagined his tongue slowly tasting her nipples.

"Damn, Mr. Sexy Ass was gentle," she moaned, massaging her breast with one hand, slowly moving the other hand between her thighs.

Massaging her engorged clitoris, as she envisioned Mr. Sexy Ass' mouth making love to her pussy, she moaned with pleasure as her fingers ventured inside her. The combination of warm water, massaging her tender nipples and her finger fucking herself, was lethal. In and out, faster and faster, until she came harder than she could remember.

Damn, she thought, as she soaked in the water, now too exhausted to move. "A mind is a terrible thing to waste!" she mumbled, followed by a relaxing chuckle.

With closed eyes, and after seconds of reclining on the bath pillow, she sat up, opened her eyes and pushed down the lever to drain the bath water. As she reclined, she almost jumped out of her skin.

Steve was standing at the bathroom door.

Chapter 8

Sitting up in the tub, Nadia had no idea how long Steve had been standing at the bathroom door. With such intensity, he stared at her through the flickering candle light. Gerald Albright was crooning in the background and the bulge in Steve's pants was huge.

Blocking the doorway, Steve seductively unzipped his pants and pulled out his dick through the opening of his blue boxers. Slowly stroking it, his dick looked like the Washington Monument. As the water was draining from the tub, Nadia felt like a prisoner. She wanted to turn the water back on and fill the tub. In her warped mind, maybe the water would protect her because she knew instinctively this was going to be one fight she wasn't going to win.

Steve walked over to her, grabbed the back of her neck and rammed his penis inside her mouth. As he gyrated with extreme force, Nadia felt she was going to choke. With his hand affixed to the back of her head, she tried pulling her head back so his manhood wouldn't pierce the back of her throat, but he wasn't having it. He wanted his dick beyond her tonsils, and if it could extend into her lungs, he would've been a much happier camper. Nadia had no choice but to get on her knees in the tub, as his forceful hold on her caused her body to twist slightly with discomfort. After a few seconds, he withdrew from her mouth and rubbed his dick all over her face, every so often beating his dick against her lips.

Nadia wanted to die.

"Get out," he demanded.

Reluctantly standing, Nadia stood before Steve naked and uncomfortable, and something in her gut told her she wasn't in for a joyful experience. Steve took her by the hand. She stepped out of the tub, and he led her into the bedroom, pushing her face down on the bed. Before Nadia knew it, Steve rammed himself into her from behind. Fucking her fiercely, Nadia felt horrible pangs in her stomach.

"Take it, bitch," he said, fucking faster and harder.

"Steve, please…"

"Shut the fuck up!"

"You're hurting me," she cried, even though his loud, animalistic grunts drowned out her cries.

As Steve was about to ejaculate, he pulled out of her, flipped her over, pulled her by the hair and forced her to her knees.

"Steve, please don't do this."

He stared down at her with much disdain, as if he hated her. "Didn't I tell you to shut the fuck up?" His scowl was replaced by a devilish grin. "Open your mouth," he ordered, tightly gripping her hair into his fist.

Doing as instructed, Nadia reluctantly parted her trembling lips.

Ramming his disgusting dick into her mouth, he stroked in and out, until he ejaculated down the back of her throat. Reflexes caused Nadia to swallow. Steve took about four more I'm-just-about-done strokes and then finally gave her mouth and throat a break.

Stunned, Nadia didn't move.

With his hands propped on his hips, he breathed heavily before escaping to the bathroom.

Nadia heard the shower and that's when the tears started. Completely numb, she felt nothing other than her knees buried into the carpet. When the shower stopped, she quickly dried her eyes and jumped in the bed under the blankets.

Steve was naked when he came out of the shower and he was dripping wet, holding his clothes in his hands. He grabbed a bottle of cologne off of the dresser and walked out of the room. Nadia wanted to cry some more, but she couldn't, as she still tasted his saltiness in her mouth. Her gums felt like rubber and the wall of her vagina felt like it was being pricked with a million tiny needles.

The urge to urinate came upon her suddenly, and she jumped up, trying to make it to the toilet before she peed on herself. Squatting, she looked between her legs. Her clitoris and labia were literally hanging. She wiped as softly as she could, washed her hands and climbed back in the bed. She lay with her back to the door, just in case Steve walked back in. She couldn't stay on her side long because her vagina was so swollen and protruding, it rubbing against the side of her leg. Nadia had no choice but to close her eyes and try not to think about her discomfort.

A few minutes later, the front door closed. Steve was gone and Nadia was in shambles, crying herself to sleep.

After eight the next morning, Nadia opened her eyes. Heaviness engulfed her and she was hurting all over. *He doesn't love me*, Nadia thought. *How could someone who loves me do what he did to me?* Nadia tried to sit up, but her shoulders and back ached. Her hair was plastered to the side of her face. Pulling back the blankets, she swung her legs over the side of the bed.

"God…" Nadia started, and then changed her mind. What was really the point? Didn't she just talk to Him, and look what happened last night anyway? Nadia knew God would never leave you, nor forsake you. She knew that if you kept your mind on Him, He would keep you in perfect peace. She knew He didn't forsake the righteous. She knew that He stayed near to the broken-hearted. She knew that weeping may endure for a night, but joy will come in the morning. She knew that her help cometh from the Lord. And, she knew her husband raped her last night.

A wave of tears gushed from her, as that harsh realization hit her. Nadia needed to get up. She went into the bathroom and looked in the mirror. She was a mess. She sat on the toilet and her stomach was in knots. And, there it was, her period, followed by terrible cramps. After she cleaned up, she got the ibuprofen from the medicine cabinet. She swallowed three tablets, with no water, and started her shower.

The water was as hot as she could stand it. Standing under the waterfall, Nadia sobbed uncontrollably, repeatedly scrubbing her skin with the exfoliating gloves, trying to remove Steve's violation. As she cleaned herself, she began to feel a little better, although her vagina was still very sore. Nadia decided she was going to church. She didn't even know if Steve was home or not, and, frankly, could care less, but she needed to do something to get herself together before picking up the kids.

Nadia got out of the shower, dried off, slipped on her underwear and a sanitary napkin. "Ouch," she cringed, as the cotton weave rubbed against her still swollen clitoris. *I hate him, I hate him, I hate him,"* Nadia thought, wrapping a towel around her. Standing in the walk-in closet, she chose the simple black dress, as it would allow her body to do the rest. The Smooth Jazz channel was still playing. Nadia grabbed the remote and turned to the Gospel channel.

"Something about the name Jesus, something about the name Jesus, it is the sweetest name I know. Oh, how I love the name Jesus…"

Standing still in the middle of the bedroom floor, Nadia allowed that song to minister to her spirit. She opened up her mouth and started singing, "Oh how I love the name Jesus." The atmosphere, to Nadia, felt like it was changing when she called on the name of Jesus. Hugging herself, she threw her head back and belted out the words, feeling them deep down in her soul. Yes, she loved Jesus!

"Where you going"? asked Steve, as he took the remote and turned off the television.

Nadia didn't open her eyes for a few seconds, as she tilted her head and looked at him out of the corner of her eye. "I'm going to praise God this morning," she said with more boldness than she thought she would.

Steve stepped very close to her and leaned in to her face. He looked her in the eye, his nose almost touching hers. "Can you fix a brother something to eat before you go hunting for deacons? Huh? Can you at least do that?"

Nadia went to the closet, grabbed her plush red robe, and put it on. She walked past Steve toward the kitchen. He was always accusing her of fucking around and she was getting tired of it. She made him a quick breakfast of grits, eggs and bacon, and secretly prayed that he would choke to death and then she could live her life.

In the ten years that Steve and Nadia were together, he never went to church with her and the kids. Nadia made up excuses as to why their father didn't go, but then they began to ask him. Nadia would just shake her head as he lied to them repeatedly about having to go to work or some crazy emergency would come up, every single Sunday. And every Sunday he would accuse her of going to church because Nadia must be cheating on him.

After plating his breakfast, Nadia walked back into the bedroom and Steve was lying on the bed.

"Come here for a second," he said.

"I'm getting dressed, Steve."

"Guess you're getting all dressed up to impress that pastor, huh? That dude got all y'all panties wet and you dumb ass women running and giving him all your money. He probably gets more pussy from you church bitches than a pimp gets from his hoes."

Nadia spun around and looked that jackass square in the eye.

"That's probably who you were thinking about while you were in the tub last night," he continued. "I bet I fixed that shit though." He laughed.

This motherfucker knew exactly what he'd done to her. *Asshole!*

"If you feel that way about me then why don't you come to church with me?"

Steve raised his eyebrows at her like she was one of the kids. "If I go, all I'm gonna do is learn the church game. You know, talk to the hearts of you emotional ass women, make you cry, console you and fuck you. And you don't want me studying that fool. I'll mess around and become a pastor." He laughed.

Nadia didn't crack a smile.

Now sitting on the edge of the bed, he continued. "And why can't you just stay here until you go get the kids?"

"I need to get to church," Nadia said.

He stood up. "Seems to me that you need to do everything, but take care of your man. He walked out of the room.

Please let him choke on that breakfast, she thought.

Brushing her hair back into a headband, she slipped on her dress, stockings and shoes. Nadia grabbed her Bible off the dresser and her long, green wool coat from the closet, and walked out into the living room where Steve sat with his feet propped up on the table, punishing his food.

Damn, he's still living, Nadia thought. "See you later," Nadia said, opening the front door.

"What are we having for dinner tonight?" he asked.

"I'm not sure. Is it possible for you to go get the kids while I'm at church?"

"If you got time to go to church, then you got time to get the kids."

With a quick roll of the eyes, Nadia slammed the door behind her.

Chapter 9

From her home, it took her about forty-five minutes to get to church. Nadia drove in complete silence. Sometimes any noise can be too much noise. Her mind kept going back to how Steve startled her when he was standing in that bathroom door, wondering how much he saw. That thought prompted her to look in her purse for Mr. Sexy Ass' card. She tore it up into little pieces and threw it out of the window. She didn't need any more drama in her life and something told her that if she inhaled Mr. Sexy Ass just a little bit now, she would be intoxicated with him later.

Pulling into the church parking lot, Nadia's stomach started cramping up from her period. She swallowed three more ibuprofens dry and sat in the parking lot for a few minutes. She leaned her head on the headrest and exhaled. Never in a million years did she imagine she would be living this kind of life. Her mother and father worked hard for her and her sister, showing them what stability was. They attended one elementary school that went from pre-kindergarten to eighth grade and one high school. They lived in one house while growing up. They had one mother and one father to raise them, not a lot of different men and women taking turns, acting as if they loved them for the moment. Stability was her life. Could that be what was working against her? Had she stayed in this mess with Steve because she was afraid of change?

Nadia got her purse and Bible and stepped out of the car. A smile graced her face, as she heard the choir singing from the parking lot, and instantly that beautiful sound put pep in her step.

Walking in the church, she was greeted by one of the young male ushers around fifteen years old. She loved to see young men doing the work of the Lord. As soon as she walked into the sanctuary, she felt the spirit of God. She was ushered to the middle of the church and thankfully, she had an end seat. She sat her purse on the pew and joined in clapping and singing with the choir and the congregation. *"Real, real...Jesus is real to me. Oh...yeah He gave her the victory...So many people doubt Him...I can't live without Him...That is why I love Him so...He's so real to me."* Each time they sung those lyrics, she realized how real God is.

At the end of the song, the church was on fire. The congregation tried to sit down, but the spirit was so high. People were rocking, clapping, and shouting "Amen and Thank you, Jesus!" The church just couldn't seem to calm down, even as Pastor Higgins stood up. Every time he tried to speak, someone would yell out in the spirit of God. Then Pastor Higgins did it!

"Somebody in this place knows that the Lord is real! Ya' see, somebody had to call on Him! I don't know who you are, but somebody done been through hell this week!"

Nadia couldn't hold it any longer! She jumped up and the Holy Spirit took over. She must've run around the church three times. Every time she thought about the goodness of God, her head went back and she ran harder. When she thought about her husband, she started wailing. When she thought about her children, she started dancing. Whew, that thang was getting good to her!

"Hallelujah," Nadia shouted. "Glory to God!" She jumped, danced and continued praising. "Hey, hey…He's worthy!" She hollered and took off running again.

Before Nadia knew it, a circle of Prayer Warriors had surrounded her and locked hands. She heard praying and moaning.

"Give it to God!" someone said.

"It's over, let it go Nadia, let it go!" prophesied another.

"Praise him, child!" came another.

Eventually, Nadia calmed down, but she was weeping uncontrollably. She fell into one of the Prayer Warriors who helped her to the nearest pew. She laid her head on the shoulder of the Prayer Warrior who wrapped her arms around Nadia. The first Prayer Warrior spoke in tongues as the other Prayer Warrior placed blessing oil on her head and hands. She took off Nadia's shoes, oiled up her feet and said, "In the name of Jesus, go forth!" After that, somebody had to run to get the Prayer Warrior!

It took nearly an hour for everything to come back to order and the regular order of service hadn't even started. Things remained steady throughout the Morning Prayer, the two songs that the choir sang and the announcements. As Nadia sat through the service, guilt invaded her. Although her husband wasn't perfect, Nadia lusted in her heart for another man. Was last night punishment for her sin? Nadia did not commit the actual act and wouldn't, but in her mind she physically felt Mr. Sexy Ass all over her. Now that she had settled down, her vagina began to ache again, a constant reminder of last night.

During the announcements, Nadia learned there would be a second service with a guest pastor from a church in Virginia. *Yes,* Nadia thought. She came for the Word and now she could get an overdose. When the announcements were over, the pastor's wife welcomed the visitors. Nadia chose this time to run to the restroom and call Steve. Her legs felt like rubber bands from all of that running and praising. Nadia used the restroom and washed her hands. She needed lotion badly, and her face had ashy, tearstains and pieces of tissue around her eyes from the Prayer Warriors blotting her face. Nadia wet a paper towel, wiped her face and took the lotion out of her purse. The light on her cell phone was blinking, which meant a call was coming through. Nadia looked at the phone. Steve.

"Hello."

"What time you coming home?"

"Well, I was getting ready to call you. There's gonna be a second service, so I might be home at around six."

Dead silence.

"Hello, Steve?"

"What the hell you mean second service and six? What am I supposed to eat?"

"Well, Ma and Daddy will feed the kids. I am going to eat here between services and I can just get you a plate from the church and bring it home."

"So, what you're saying is you're not cooking tonight?"

That heart palpitating anxious feeling came over her again. Nadia didn't say anything.

"You can run to that church, get all dressed up for the men in there and all I ask is for my wife to fix me a hot meal for dinner and you can't do that?"

"Steve, I'm going to bring you something home. It's just…"

Click!

I hate him, I hate him, I hate him. Wait a minute she was in church. She almost called him back, but the devil wasn't going to deter her from hearing the Word.

She put her phone back in her purse and hurried back to the sanctuary. Just as Nadia was walking in, the pastor was giving the scripture that he was going to preach from for his sermon.

"Everyone please stand and turn with me to Romans 12: 2. When you have it, say Amen."

After a few seconds, all were standing and "Amen" echoed throughout the sanctuary.

Pastor Higgins said, "I am going to read it aloud and you all read it to yourselves."

Pastor threw his shoulders back. He elevated his voice to BOOM and began to read.

"Do not conform any longer to the pattern of this world, but be transformed by the renewing of your mind. Then you will be able to test and approve what God's will is, His good, pleasing and perfect will. Let me focus on, but be *transformed*. Church, I said transformed! By the renewing of your mind! Brothers and sistahs, our subject for today will be: It's Time to be Free From the Jail of Your Mind."

Another round of "Amen" and "Preach Pastor" came from the congregation.

No wonder the enemy was trying to get her to come home. Satan knew that Nadia needed to hear this. She laughed to herself as she realized the devil was indeed real, too.

"So, you think you're free?" Pastor Higgins asked the congregation.

From there, Pastor preached on how many people are incarcerated by their thinking. He spoke on how nothing is left to the imagination in this new age of technology and you have to be extremely strong, mentally, to resist the devil. He went on to say the Word is what is needed to maintain a strong, healthy, positive mind. Sexual images, gossip, slander and multiple sins are at our fingertips and we have to deny ourselves and resist the urge to sin.

Then Pastor Higgins came into her world.

"Some of y'all are in jail in your relationships. Not because that man or that woman is holding you there, but because mentally, you're choosing to live there."

She couldn't look up because Nadia felt like Pastor Higgins would be looking directly at her and she hadn't uttered a word to him about her home life.

"Slavery is over and some of y'all might as well walk around shackled and chained. You know you should be Kunta, but you're settling for being Toby. *You* imprison yourselves and you give the other person in the relationship the key to unlock you.

"Some of y'all are with somebody just to have somebody. You've given somebody the reigns to your life and you let them steer you in whatever direction they want you to go. If the person pulls you to the right, then you have their permission to be happy. If they pull you to the left, then they're telling you that you're going to be sad. Let me elaborate on that. If they're happy, then you can be happy. If they're angry, then your day is bad. If they call you then you can function. If they don't call you, you can't get out of the bed. Church, let me ask you something? Did God choose the person you're with or did you choose the person you're with?"

"Ouch, Pastor!" Nadia said quietly. "Please get off my toes!"

"Your destiny is in your hands and it starts with how you think. What do you think of yourself? Do you enjoy having someone barking orders at you like you weren't a whole person before you met them? Let me ask you something else?"

"Come on with it, Pastor," said someone from the back of the church.

"Are you afraid to be free or do you have a slave mentality in your relationship?"

There was murmuring all over the church. A few people jumped to their feet, but Nadia just sat in awe of that burning question. Pastor Higgins preached for about an hour. Even after Pastor finished preaching, Nadia sat thinking on that question during the "Call to Christ" and the benediction.

After the first service, Nadia went outside to use her phone to call her parents and let them know she would be a little late. She noticed that she had a text from Steve. The text simply read: *You ain't shit.*

Again, Nadia almost called, but why? It was going to be a fight and her stomach was cramping anyway. She wasn't in the mood for his mess and with her period and that lingering question, Nadia decided to leave it alone.

After calling her parents, she walked back into the dining area of the church to buy two dinners. Nadia brought Steve smothered chicken, macaroni and cheese, mustard greens and cornbread, and a slice of lemon pound cake, which he absolutely loved.

"Maybe this will smooth things over a little bit," Nadia figured to herself as she realized her bank account was getting lower.

She sat down and ate with some of her friends. They were going on and on about how they weren't slaves to anybody and they knew they were free.

Yeah right, Nadia thought. One thing that Nadia learned is that the one thing that people claim not to be is exactly what they are. She didn't say anything though. She just listened. She had so much on her plate and Pastor Higgins gave her so much to ponder.

Nadia often wondered how many people did what the pastor said or did they just enjoy warming the pews Sunday after Sunday, running, shouting, hollering, screaming and then go right back to the same mess they'd just prayed to God to release them from. *So, how much is this us being out of the will of God and not listening to Him when He tells us, "No?"* Naturally, people don't want to hear no, especially if they are not accustomed to denying themselves, so they revert to their old ways, getting mad at their lives because they chose not to listen. Just as Nadia did when she chose to marry Steve.

She ate, listened to a few more lies at the table, and then Nadia decided to go back to the sanctuary and wait for the second service. She thought about how she was running around this holy place this morning and now she was filled with shame and fear. How was that possible? Where was her faith? Did this mean she doesn't believe as she should or is there something wrong with her? A spiritual war was raging inside of her, and she needed to release these thoughts. Nadia opened up her notebook.

"After the Shout"

Whatchu gonna do after the shout?
Heard all the things Pastor preached about

Almost half the church was laid on out
But when you got up, you were still filled with doubt

Had the whole church jumpin' up on their feet
Singin' and clappin' feeling almost complete
But when the music stopped and Pastor took his seat
The devil crept in and you felt the heat

Left church singin' a brand new tune
Gonna get free from jail real, real soon
By the time the sun turned into the moon
Your dreams became as funny as a cartoon

The enemy is laughing right in your face
Because he watched you shout all over the place
While you've been hollerin', "I've been saved by grace"
Your dreams and visions were vanishing without a trace

So whatchu gonna do after the shout?
Faith without works is dead, so should we go out
And purchase your casket while you're in this drought
Or get up and do what Pastor Higgins was talkin' bout

Don't give power to the enemy
Take back your life in the name of JC
Say to God, "Lord, what do you want from me?"
And then begin to walk in your destiny

So whatchu gonna do after the shout?
Get up, get free and start movin' about
Pray without ceasing day in and day out
And move into your purpose after you fall out!

"Go head, girl! I ministered to myself on this one," Nadia said, laughing out loud.

"What you laughing at?" asked Theresa.

"Girl, when you get here?"

"I just walked in," she said, taking a seat next to her. "How was service this morning?" She took off her coat. That girl had a shape on her. She had curves for days. And, the deacon in the pew a few seats behind them must've realized it because he came over to them.

"Service was great," Nadia said.

"Sho' was," said Deacon Nasty. Nadia didn't know where he came from. Deacon Nasty was about five feet tall, one hundred ten pounds and smelled like he bathed in cologne that made her eyes water. His hair was parted on the left and slicked down with what looked to be a gallon of Vaseline. Although he was as skinny as a pencil, he was sweating profusely and his front tooth was chipped and outlined with something brown.

"God is so good," he said to Theresa with open arms for a nice hug.

Nadia waited to see what Theresa was going to do. Nadia loved how she handled herself in these situations.

"Dude, put your arms down. I don't know you."

Nadia couldn't help it, as she burst out laughing while he stood there looking cheap and lowering his arms slowly.

"And yes, the Lord is good," she said as she sat down beside Nadia.

They looked at Deacon Nasty as he cleared his throat, popped his collar and pimped away. Now they were in hysterics. Nadia needed that laugh; she had too much going on mentally and that joke of a man was timely.

Theresa smirked. "These men kill me, using church as a playground to meet vulnerable women."

"Ain't it the truth," Nadia agreed.

Nadia turned and looked at Theresa, narrowing her eyes and then she made her voice as deep as she could, and said mockingly, "What's wrong, sistah? Come on and talk to me, baby. It's my duty as a deacon to help you. Now what's the problem?" Nadia tried not to laugh.

"Well," Theresa said, playing along. "My man ain't doing me right."

"Ah, that's a shame," Nadia said, placing her arm around Theresa.

"Just give me your number and I'll make sure to come and do you right."

They broke into laughter, but stopped as people walked into the sanctuary for the second service.

The second service lasted for about an hour and a half. Afterwards, Nadia hugged Theresa, grabbed Steve's food and headed to her car to get her children. Nadia learned a lot today and that question was still burning in her mind.

Is she afraid to be free?

Chapter 10

As Nadia drove toward her parents' house, she pondered over her life. She thought about her baby sitter, Mama Carla—who was rather elderly and, now that she thought it about, seemed too old to be caring for children—and how she had her first sexual experience under Mama Carla's care. Mama Carla had two teen-aged grandsons—Ricky and Al—who were around thirteen or so, and used to take turns laying on top of Nadia and gyrating with their clothes on. At such a tender age, she was very confused about what was going on and why they were moving that way on top of her, and sweating so much.

One memory, in particular, will forever be etched in her mind. It was when the oldest grandson made her go to the bathroom with him. He made her squat over the toilet seat, he put his penis very close to her young vagina, and they peed together. She hated going there, but she never told her mother or father.

Nadia had very similar experiences with another sitter who lived across the street from her elementary school. She was in the second grade and a boy at the sitter, Tron, was in the sixth grade. He used to wait until their babysitter went to sleep before he would make her take down her pants and feel around on her young vagina. Nadia's premature body betrayed her and she liked the feeling. After he violated her young place, she wondered why she didn't want him touching her anymore. Now that she was grown, she understood that she was having an orgasm. She also knew what he was doing to her was wrong. She thought he was a nice looking boy and if she let him touch her then he would like her. That wasn't the case at all. If he were feeling nastier than normal, he would make her lie down on the couch and rub his penis around in her vagina. He violated her private places daily and when he was done, he wouldn't utter two words to her.

There were other kids there, too, and Nadia wasn't sure if they were also being molested. As he talked and played with them, she thought that maybe they weren't. She would try to play with him, but he would call her "Tar Baby" or "Ugly Girl," and she would be devastated. But, the next day he would molest her and ignore her again. She would try harder to make him like her, but it never worked. Hence, she learned the art of trying to make people who hurt her love her.

Being a dark-skinned, flat chested, bow-legged, girl starving for attention made life hard for her. Today, Nadia felt her complexion was a blessing, but it seemed to be a curse in her youth. Although she had a head full of thick hair, her mother always made her wear it in cornrows. She preferred nice, long bangs, but her mother said she needed to grow to appreciate things in life and bangs would make her too grown too soon. Nadia now wondered what her mother would think if she knew how wearing cornrows didn't stop her early sexual experiences. That thought made Nadia realize that with Darryl and Danielle, she had to pay attention to more than the visual. She made a mental note to study her children's behavior and not let them be exposed to what she experienced. Repeated molestations.

Nadia's negative, over-pleasing type of thinking spilled over into her relationships very early on. She got her first boyfriend in the seventh grade, and she was head over heels in love with him. He constantly gawked at other girls and had the nerve to talk to her about how pretty they were. She was always extremely uncomfortable when he started in on those disrespectful conversations, but she tried to play it off, and she never left him. She went out of her way to do things for him like buy him stuff from the candy store so he would say some of those nice things about her, too, but he didn't.

Nadia's high school boyfriend was about the same. He cheated on her, yet she tried to make him love her by ignoring his scandalous ways, and doing whatever he wanted her to do. She took her dysfunctional mindset to college, and her boyfriend there impregnated another girl. His reward for fucking over her was clothes, cologne and a leather jacket for Christmas. Yes, she tried to make him love her, too. The few boyfriends she had in her life, she tried pleasing them all. Nowhere in Nadia's life did it seem that she had the time or the knowledge of how to love Nadia.

And, to top it off, Nadia met and married Steve. Initially, he was very chivalrous. He always opened doors for her, they held hands when they went out, and when she went to his parents' house—where he lived at the time—he would fix her dinner. He just seemed like a man who needed a little extra love and because he gave her a little more attention than the others did, she latched on.

Sure, there were early signs, but when you're dating, one has no idea how these little things will manifest later. Steve and Nadia dated three years before she fucked up and walked down the aisle. She ignored a clear red flag early in the third year of their marriage. She had to have two small fibroids removed during an in-and-out surgery. That same night after the surgery, when she was resting and recovering in the bedroom, Steve crawled into bed behind her and wrapped his arms around her. It felt so good, especially because she was so tired. Holding her, she could feel his erection through his pants as he slowly dry humped her butt. Then he moved his hands up toward her breast and started squeezing as he was licking in her ear. She was frozen with disbelief. She didn't move, but she said, "I can't tonight. I don't feel good." Steve got up without a word, and slept on the couch. And not a damn thing has changed.

So now, Nadia was in a marriage she knew was toxic, yet she wouldn't leave. Why? Fear? Yes, fear. Did having a man in her life mean that she would not be alone? She sure felt alone in every relationship that she'd ever had. And she felt alone now. That's why Mr. Sexy Ass was such great company.

Pulling up into her parents' driveway, she saw her father standing outside talking with the kids. She got out of the car and walked toward them.

"Hi, Mommy," the kids said, as they raced to the car. They liked to see who could get their seatbelt on the quickest.

"How was service?" her father asked.

"It was great. Actually, both services were great. I have a lot to think about."

He reached in his pocket and pulled out a one hundred dollar bill. "Here you go, baby. I hit the number and this is a little something for you."

"Thank you so much, Daddy." She gave him a great, big hug.

He walked her to her car and opened the door for her. "I love all of y'all," he said.

"We love you, too," Nadia and the kids said in unison.

Before Nadia pulled off, she put the one hundred dollar bill in her wallet behind her driver's license. She didn't want Steve to know she had any extra money or it would surely be gone. This money would help her through the week since she was just about broke, no thanks to Steve's ungrateful ass.

The kids were in the back seat playing My Car Click Click. When you see a nice car you say, "My car click click." The click represents the sound a key makes when something is being locked. That way when you have called the car and locked it, it is your car. Heaven forbid if you don't say, "Click." Someone can take your car, "click" it and it's theirs.

As they were playing that rather annoying game, her mind went back to her past as she was trying to understand her fear of leaving Steve. Of course, she's thought about it hundreds of times, but the act of really doing it just seemed so farfetched. She listened to Danielle's voice in the back seat. Knowing her daughter watched her closely in the house, she also knew her son watched his father as well. The thought that her son might end up like his father was scary. Likewise, she had to make sure Danielle didn't become a doormat for any man, even though Nadia was clearly exhibiting that behavior right before Danielle's eyes.

"I declare right now in the precious name of Jesus that Darryl will not be like his father and Danielle will not waddle in self-hate, but will love herself," she said out loud, but not loud enough for the kids to hear. She looked at them through the rear view mirror, smiled and headed to the Plantation.

When they pulled up to the house, Steve's car sat in the driveway. Nadia was really hoping he wouldn't be home. Sighing heavily, she grabbed his food and prepared herself for drama.

When they walked into the house, Steve was lying on the couch watching television.

"Hi, Daddy," Danielle said, as she ran over and kissed him on the cheek.

"What's up, Pops?" Darryl said, laughing.

That put a smile on Steve's face. "What's happening, son?" He gave Darryl five.

"Go put your things up and get ready for your baths. School tomorrow," Nadia instructed.

"Awwww," they both cried.

"Hey, baby," Nadia said, walking over to Steve. "I brought you some food."

"I told you I wanted you to cook me a meal," he said not taking his eyes off the television.

She was so tired from her long day; she just knew Steve wasn't suggesting she prepare a meal, especially when she spent money on food.

"Steve, I have food for you right here. I got you dessert, too."

Steve sat up and turned down the volume on the television. "I said I want you to cook me a meal."

"Steve, I'm cramping from my period and I've had a long day. I really need to get some rest."

"You know, it amazes me how you always need rest after you've done everything that you want to do."

Nadia didn't respond.

Not in the mood for what he was surely about to bring, she walked into the kitchen and started dinner for him. She removed frozen chicken wings from the freezer and put them in water. She walked to the back of the house and got the kids' pajamas and clothes ready for school. She ran Danielle's bathwater in her bathroom and Darryl's bathwater in the main hallway bathroom. She then returned to the kitchen, seasoned the thawed chicken and put it in the oven. She boiled a pot of rice and steamed broccoli. Dinner was fixed and the kids were taken care of all within the time span of about an hour.

"Your dinner's ready," she said, walking past him and into Danielle's room. Darryl was in there and they were waiting for her to pray with them.

"I want to pray," Darryl said.

"Okay, go ahead, son."

"Mom, are you serious?" Danielle pleaded.

"Danny, if your brother wants to pray, then he can pray."

Danielle sighed heavily and they clasped hands and bowed heads. Nadia knew what was coming, but even Darryl's long prayer was better than looking at their nothing-ass father.

"Dear Lord, thank you for being God. And thank you for sending Your son Jesus to die for our sins. Please let us be nice to everybody. Please help Mommy and Daddy and Danny and me and Grandma and Granddaddy and my teacher and dogs and cats and Obama and…" Darryl looked around. "Thank you for the door and," he paused, looking around some more, "…and the bed and the wall and the window and the television." He looked at Nadia's hand. "And rings and nails and watches…" Darryl went on for a good three minutes thanking God for anything he could see. Danielle couldn't take anymore.

"In Jesus name we pray, Amen," Danielle loudly interjected.

"Dang, I wasn't finished," Darryl said, walking to his room.

"Another day you'll be able to finish," Nadia said, rubbing the back of her neck that had started to ache from having it bent for so long.

"Good night, babies." Nadia kissed Danielle and went to Darryl's room to kiss him.

She walked into the living room and Steve was still seated on the couch. She fixed him a plate and brought it to him.

"I don't want that," he said.

"Huh?"

"You ain't put no love in that meal."

"Steve, I don't know what you're talking about. I brought you food from church and you didn't want that, then I fixed you dinner and now you're saying you don't want it because I didn't put love into it. I just don't understand."

"What I'm saying is if you would've stayed here today, you wouldn't have thrown together this meal. You would've put some effort into it. But you come in here and throw this shit together and bring it to me like you did something big."

"Steve, I fixed this for you because you asked me to."

"Exactly. Because I asked you to. I shouldn't have had to ask you. You eat this shit. I'll be back after I get me something to eat." He got up, got his jacket and stormed out of the house.

Nadia sat on the couch and stared at ESPN. She wanted to shower and try to get herself together, but she couldn't. She felt paralyzed. She managed to get up and go to her room. She lay across the bed and chanted, "*I hate him, I hate him, I hate him.*"

After she'd fallen asleep for a few hours, she was awakened by a fit of cramping. She willed herself to rise up and move toward the dresser for the ibuprofen in the bottom of her purse. Arching her back, and stretching out her arms, she headed for the kitchen for water. When she came upon the living room, two black women licked each other's vaginas on the television while Steve was stretched out on the couch. He didn't see her though, as she stepped back quickly and watched him. He was masturbating furiously. He was so into stroking himself that he didn't even notice the presence of his wife. She was simply disgusted. Before she turned to walk away, she noticed a

McDonald's bag and drink on the living room table. She went back to her bedroom and swallowed the pills dry, not thinking that she could've gotten water from the bathroom in her room.

Well, she thought. *At least he's not bothering me.*

Chapter 11

Everything Nadia had been going through at home must have been showing on her face the next day at work.

"You look like you've been hit by a truck," Theresa said, biting into her bologna and cheese sandwich, as she and Nadia were having lunch in the library.

"I feel like shit," Nadia said, sipping on water.

Mr. Lowe walked in. "Mind if I join y'all?"

"Come on in," Theresa said.

Mr. Lowe joined them at the round table. "What's wrong with you?" he asked Nadia, with much concern.

Nadia couldn't hold it in any longer. She told them everything. Neither one of them touched their food, as they hung on her every word. Nadia felt so much better releasing her life. Maybe it was a cry for help, but she couldn't be sure. She wasn't sure about anything in her life anymore.

"Why don't you just take the rest of the day off," suggested Mr. Lowe.

"And why would I want to go home?"

"Damn, I'm sorry," he said.

"On Sunday, Pastor Higgins asked us do we have a slave mentality when it comes to our relationships, meaning are we scared to leave."

"So are you?" Theresa asked.

"I must be because I'm still there."

"Let me let you ladies in on a little secret," said Mr. Lowe. "Men sense fear like dogs. We know when you're afraid or too insecure to leave us. Our egos don't just fall upon us. Women help us to build them up all the time."

"Please explain that to me." Nadia was eager to hear his point.

"We can tell when we have a woman that is scared to leave us or is very insecure."

Theresa and Nadia both sat up in their seats.

"I know that it sounds terrible, but once we know that we have you in that way, we get comfortable because we know that you aren't going anywhere. That's about the time that we just do things to see what we can get away with."

"I should slap the shit out of you," Theresa said, without cracking a smile.

"Don't get mad at me," Mr. Lowe said. "I'm letting you in on some things to help you. I'm mad as hell right now for Nadia, but it's her life and she has to make some decisions."

Nadia knew he spoke the truth, but it was still painful to hear.

"So what type of shit do y'all start doing to see if you can get away with?" asked a very irritated Theresa.

"It might be that we say something out of the way to you and then watch how you react to it. Or we might not call you for a few days and watch what you do. We're training you early."

Now Nadia was ready to slap the shit out of him.

"So," he continued, "If you don't put us back in line or let us know that you think more of yourself than what we're giving you, well, we know that you want a man so bad that you will just take it. However, the woman that is assertive and has boundaries is the one that we respect and chase."

"See, that's why I won't call Thomas my man," said Theresa. "That brother gotta earn that title."

"You're right," agreed Mr. Lowe. "It's nothing wrong with making a man work or telling him no. The problem is that many women are afraid that if they do that then the man will not want her anymore. We play the ratio card all the time and let you know that another one's waiting right behind you."

"It's all a game?" Nadia shook her head in disgust. "A fucking game!"

"Listen, Nadia. You told Steve how to treat you a long time ago by making him a god in your life. You can blame him all you want, but this is your fault. He's only been able to do to you what you have allowed him to do. If you would've told him 'No' a long time ago, you might have lost him, but you wouldn't be sitting here feeling the way you do either."

Tears welled in Nadia's eyes. She had to get herself together because she had students coming in about ten minutes. Mr. Lowe was right and that hurtful truth was burning.

"Don't cry," Theresa, said pulling Nadia to her.

"Fuck that," Mr. Lowe said. "Cry, get the shit out and then practice saying 'NO!' That motherfucker is doing whatever he wants to with your body and treating you with the utmost disrespect. You're showing your daughter a weak-ass mother who will take anything and you're showing your son that it's okay to treat women that way because his mother didn't leave. If you think that your kids don't know that something is wrong in that house, then you're crazy."

"Damn, lighten up," Theresa interjected.

"No he's right," Nadia said. "He's right."

Mr. Lowe softened. "Nadia, I'm only telling you this because I love you, but I can't listen to stuff like this and not speak my peace. I would be less of a friend to not give it to you straight and let you keep living like this. Now, there's nothing else I can do for you other than give you some Kleenex. The rest is up to you." Mr. Lowe got up, kissed Nadia on the cheek and walked out of the library.

"Are you gonna be all right?" Theresa asked her with concern.

"Yes I will be fine. I just have so much to think about."

"You know I'm here if you need me. I have to go and get my kids now, but we can talk later. Love you, girl." She gave Nadia a huge hug.

"I love you, too, Theresa. And thank you for always being there."

"You're more than welcome." She smiled, as she walked out the door.

For a brief moment, Nadia felt a bit panicky.

"No weapon formed against me shall prosper," she said out loud. She dried her eyes, rolled on fresh lip-gloss and waited for her students to arrive.

"Someday, Nadia gon'be free," she said out loud in her slavery voice. Nadia laughed and it felt good.

Chapter 12

Steve seemed to be in a good mood when Danielle and Nadia arrived home. It was no problem for him to pick up Darryl since the aftercare had already been taken care of. That, along with everything else still bothered Nadia who had been thinking about what Mr. Lowe said earlier. It's amazing how confident you can feel when you are faced with your challenges. Nadia knew what she wanted to do, but her confidence just fizzled like a fart into thin air.

"Hi, Mommy" Darryl said, hugging her waist.

"Hey, baby," Nadia said.

"He ain't a baby," Steve said.

"He's my baby," Nadia said, bending down to hug him.

Danielle walked into the kitchen.

"Now here's daddy's girl," Steve said, pulling Danielle close.

"She's a mommy's girl first," Nadia said.

"What do you mean by that?" Steve asked.

Nadia stared at him.

"Y'all go get started on your homework," Steve told the kids.

The kids ran off.

"Now what do you mean she's a mommy's girl first?" he adamantly asked.

Admittedly, Steve does have a soft spot for Danielle, his pride and joy. Nadia wondered if he ever thought that she might get a man in her life that treated her like he treated her. Nadia prayed that would never happen, but she also realized she needed to break the curse.

"What I'm saying is that sometimes you get mad and walk out of the house. At that moment, I don't know if you're coming back or not. And when you leave, you leave us all."

"Are you talking about because I went to McDonald's the other day? That was your fault."

"No, I'm not talking about that. I'm saying that every time you leave, you don't take one of the kids with you. I don't have that option and I would never walk out of the house and leave my kids."

Nadia couldn't believe what she was hearing, let alone saying. Maybe Mr. Lowe's disciplinary talk had gotten to her after all. She stepped past Steve and opened the freezer to take out the steaks. She could feel his eyes on her back.

"Who you been talking to?" he asked.

"What do you mean?"

"Some muthafucka in your head. You ain't never said no shit like that to me before."

"I haven't been talking to anybody. I was just thinking about..."

"Mommy," Danielle yelled from her room. "Darryl won't listen to me."

"Let me go and check on them," Nadia said and walked passed Steve.

"Yeah, you better go do something," he said as if Nadia was one of their children.

Nadia didn't feel like scolding Darryl, but she knew that she had to correct him. "You listen to Danielle or you are going to bed thirty minutes earlier than usual. Do I make myself clear?"

With a lowered head, he nodded. He didn't want that and he straightened up quickly.

When Nadia walked back into the kitchen, Steve was seated at the table, texting and smiling

"You know what?" he said, seeming to have forgotten about their little discussion. "Malik and Karen are always going at it."

"Why do you say that?" she asked, seasoning the steak and glad that the focus had been taken off them and onto someone else.

"Karen called me at work today and we talked for about an hour. She is so sick of Malik."

What the fuck, Nadia thought. *Why in the hell was Malik's wife calling Steve?*

"What do you mean she's sick of Malik?"

Steve's mood seemed to change so much so that it was scary. It's amazing how pleasant he became when talking about Karen.

"She was just going on and on about how she's not attracted to him anymore. Even though he works out at the gym and all of that, she said that now that they're married she lost something for him."

Nadia washed four potatoes and started wrapping them in foil.

Steve and Malik had been friends for years, but Malik had only been married for about six months. Steve told Nadia about the woman that Malik had met when they were at the sports bar having a few drinks and she walked in with her girls. Steve said that Karen was interested in him at first, but when he told her that he was married, she moved on to Malik.

"Really," Nadia responded, appearing to be so deep into potato wrapping that she hardly gave his words a second thought.

"Yeah, she was saying that she doesn't even want to sleep with him anymore. The crazy thing is that when I went to play ball with that fool the other day all he talked about was Karen. And, when we went out later, women were coming on to him all night long and he pushed them all away. His dumb ass don't even know his wife don't want him anymore." Steve laughed. "She said that she's thinking about leaving him because she don't think that this life is for her, and that when they're having sex she feels disgusted and she just wants him to hurry up. Yo', that dude is a fool!"

Damn, that bitch is real comfortable with my husband.

"Well, why is she calling you telling you all of this?"

"She just told me that she needed someone to confide in and she thought of me. Plus she said that she felt that she could trust me. You know how I am, I don't tell nobody's business and since she felt that way, I let her tell me. I'm only telling you because you're my wife and I know that you don't run your mouth."

"So what advice did you give her?"

"Shit, I didn't give her any advice. I just listened and thought about how fucked up their household is. He loves the hell out of her and she can't stand his ass. But he's always talking about how sexy she is because she got them big ass titties. He tells me how he always sucking on them babies and now I'm just laughing at him."

Nadia turned and looked at him. Steve was grinning from ear to ear like he hit the lottery or something.

"I'll be right back, I have to go to the bathroom," Steve said.

Nadia could've sworn that when Steve pulled the chair back and stood up from the table he had an erection that looked like a lamppost in his pants.

Wow, she thought. *Talking about Karen's titties did all that to you, huh?*

He walked out of the kitchen and the hurt began to settle. Yes, she was feeling something, but she couldn't be sure of what it was. Steve was terrible to her, so why did she feel the way that she did? She decided at that moment that she didn't want to hurt. So she went to the justification station.

Chill out, she silently told herself. *Your husband came and confided in you. He can't help that she called him and he really didn't do anything wrong. And, how do you know that erection was about Karen? He always wants sex and he knows you're on your period, so get that Karen bullshit out of your head!* And just like that, she felt better.

Nadia continued with dinner, wondering what was taking Steve so long. Preparing a salad, she sliced tomatoes, onions, cut cucumbers and lettuce. Finally, after about fifteen minutes Steve returned, sat down and continued talking about Malik and Karen.

"I told her that I would talk to Malik about them coming over this weekend. She said that she's so sick of him that she doesn't even want to ride in the same car with him. She's just turned off by him I guess."

"Why did you do that?" Nadia asked.

"Well, we have been friends for a long time and maybe if they come over here and sit and talk then things might get better for them."

"Well it doesn't sound like you care whether or not if things get better since you're laughing at him. It sounds to me like she is punishing him for loving her."

"Damn, you know how to fuck up a good story. I wasn't telling you all of this for you to get philosophical on me. I just wanted to rap to my lady about what's going on with my man."

"You're right baby. I'm sorry."

"I didn't ask for your opinion I just needed your ear."

"I said you're right."

Steve sighed in disgust and seemed to be sending a few texts from his phone. Nadia turned her attention to the food and wondered why she was always making an ass of herself.

Danielle sauntered into the kitchen. "Mommy, is the food ready?"

Nadia looked at her and wondered how long she had been standing there.

"In about twenty more minutes, baby. I will call you both when it's ready."

"Okay," she said and walked back down the hallway.

Steve stopped texting and looked at Nadia. Whatever mood he was in seemed to vanish.

"Baby, can you whip us up something good to eat this weekend? We can watch the game and just have a good time. Oh and see if your parents can watch the kids."

"Sure. No problem."

Steve got up from the table and walked over to Nadia. "I'm one lucky ass man," he said. Nadia relaxed a little bit and was just glad that he wasn't angry or annoyed at that moment. "I'm so glad that I don't have a woman that will call another dude and talk that kind of shit about her man. Karen's cool, but she's trifling as hell to tell me all of her business like that. My man has a grimy broad on his hands." Steve kissed her on the cheek and headed for the living room to take his position on the couch. Nadia felt an awkward sense of peace. Her period meant that she had some time to rest and he didn't feel the need to bother her.

About a half hour later, the family sat around the table and ate dinner. Afterwards, Nadia cleaned the kitchen, checked the kids' homework, prepared their baths, read them a story, prayed with them and tucked them into their beds. Steve was on the couch with the remote and his cell phone and seemed to be very comfortable.

It was a little after nine and Nadia was exhausted, and she hadn't peed since she'd gotten home earlier that evening. Sauntering into the bathroom, she stood in front of the mirror and peered at her reflection. She looked stressed. She sat down on the toilet...

〜 〜 〜

"Nadia, Nadia!" Steve was banging on the door. "What in the hell are you doing in there?"

"Huh?" She fell asleep on the toilet. She leaned forward and opened the door.

"Girl, it's almost twelve o'clock. How long have you been in here?"

Nadia was out of it.

"That don't make no damn sense," Steve said and closed the door.

Nadia cleaned herself and washed her hands. That was a first and a real sign that her body needed rest.

Without showering, Nadia climbed in the bed and silently thanked God that her flow was keeping that man away from her tonight.

Chapter 13

It was Friday, and most people are excited for the weekend. However, Nadia didn't give damn. Her week went the same as it usually did, except her menstruation was a deterrent from Steve. Now that her period was over, Nadia's life was backwards. She was the only woman in the world who was saddened at the end of her menstrual cycle. Like anyone who lived for the weekend, Nadia dreaded it, as going to work every day was a vacation from her life with Steve.

However, she did have one, little, inkling of joy. She managed to hold on to the one-hundred-dollar bill her father had given her. She figured after church next Sunday she would stop off at the mall and buy a little dress, a pair of shoes, a lip-gloss, just something to make her feel better. It's amazing how one can hold on to their last little bit of money forever.

After picking up Danielle, Nadia was on her way to pick up Darryl when her cell phone rang. Looking at caller ID, she smiled as she answered the phone.

"Hey, Daddy."

"Hey, baby. What time are you bringing the kids over?"

"Well, I have Danny and I'm on my way to get Darryl now. I should be there in about an hour or so."

"All right. I'll see y'all when you get here," he said, hanging up before she could say good-by.

She laughed.

"What are you laughing at, Mommy?" Danielle asked.

"Your silly grandfather."

"Oh, well I like it when you laugh, Mommy."

Turning down the radio, Nadia looked at Danielle through the rearview mirror. "Why did you say that?" she asked, fearing what her answer might be.

"I just don't really see you laugh or smile. You always look so tired. Do you love Daddy?"

Fuck no, Nadia thought, wanting to scream it from the highest mountaintop, but didn't dare say out loud. *Why is she asking me this?*

Taking a deep breath before responding, Nadia had to remember that Danielle was her child and not her friend. Obviously, she witnessed some things and she didn't need the weight of this shitty ass marriage on her young shoulders. With all she had in her, Nadia refrained from saying, "Baby, *fuck* your daddy. I'm picking up Darryl and we're never going back home!"

However, that would have been inappropriate and probably would have caused the child much turmoil, so she changed her train of thought.

"Yes, I do love your father. Why did you ask me that?'

"Well, if you love him and he loves you then why don't y'all do something to make you laugh?"

Oh, you mean like watch the nigga choke? Nadia's thoughts were a little much today.

"Okay, baby. Maybe we can."

"Yes!" Danielle exclaimed, as she sat back and acted as if she had just solved every problem concerning world peace.

They picked up Darryl and headed toward her parents' house. Cooking for Malik and Karen this weekend was the last thing she felt like doing, as all week long she'd hoped that somehow plans would change, but then how would that be good for her? Girlfriend was damned if she did, damned if she didn't. *I guess this is the prison that Pastor Higgins was talking about,* she thought, feeling like she was walking into brick walls no matter which way she turned.

"My red corvette, click click," Darryl shouted.

"That ain't nothing," Nadia said. "My black Porsche, click click."

"Where?" Darryl exclaimed.

Well, Danielle wanted to see her mother laugh, so why not join in this silly game. "I see it, I see it!" hollered Danielle.

"Aw man!" said Darryl, now more determined than ever to find a better car than the car Nadia found.

"Your brown station wagon, click click," Darryl said to Danielle.

"Eww, I don't want that."

"Too bad; I clicked it for you and now it's yours!"

That brown station wagon led to a fifteen-minute argument that ended as they pulled into her parents' driveway. After her father retrieved the kids from the car, she kissed them both, and headed home.

While driving, thoughts of her day invaded her mind. She popped in a smooth jazz CD, letting her mind wander. Theresa and Mr. Lowe checked in on her every day since she confessed about her home drama. Earlier, the three of them had lunch and she told them about Malik and Karen coming for dinner.

"Something about what he's telling you about his best friend and his best friend's wife just doesn't sound right to me," said Mr. Lowe, shaking his head. "Nadia you have to learn to listen to people. Always remember this, there's a whole lot behind a little bit."

"What do you mean by that?" she asked.

"Well, what I mean is that people will always tell you what they're doing. All you have to do is listen. People talk about what is dear to them. They can't help it. So, it's just my opinion, but I think that your husband is talking about this Karen because, well, he can't help it."

Intently, Nadia listened to Mr. Lowe, but she wasn't trying to hear what he was saying. It was too much and it was putting her in an uncomfortable place. However, she had to admit; it stung and maybe it stung because there was a ring of truth to what he was saying.

Mr. Lowe continued. "Baby, I don't know what it's going to take for you to learn, but maybe you're just one of those people who feels some sort of crazy love from this dysfunction. You seem to be one of those people who function in drama. Perhaps a normal life is what you think you want, but drama is where you feel most comfortable."

Theresa chimed in. "Did you say the nigga had an erection after he finished talking about her? So, he probably left you to go jack off, then came back, and finished the conversation like it was nothing? Fuck that shit!"

Perplexed and speechless, Nadia simply hung her head in shame.

Theresa and Mr. Lowe shared a look of silent confirmation of them agreeing about their feelings on her life. How Nadia was living made absolutely no sense to them. Maybe she was burdening them with her drama and the fact that she wasn't making any power moves. Talk about tough love. She definitely got a dose of that today.

How much of her life has to pass by before she realized what she needed to do? She knew that what Pastor Higgins said was right, and as much as it pained her to admit it, even to herself, she knew that Mr. Lowe was right, too.

As Nadia pulled up to the house, Steve's car was gone. *God is good!* She walked into the house and sat down on the couch. She was exhausted, as she looked around and wondered what it would be like if she lived alone, just she and the kids and no Steve. Hell, Steve hadn't even been picking up Darryl lately. He doesn't cook. He lay around while she cleaned the house. Did she really need him? He's not even a warm body at night. She cringed when he touched her and loved it when he wasn't around. *So why the fuck am I staying?*

Because your dumb ass loves drama, said some strange voice in her head.

Kicking off her shoes, she snuggled up on the couch. That mental picture of Steve masturbating on this same couch made her nauseous. She quickly threw that thought out of her mind and thought about Mr. Sexy Ass. *Now how sad is that?* She met the man one time and now she was about to have a mental affair with him. If she hadn't torn up that number, would she have called him? Of course not, as cheating wasn't in her nature, but it was exciting to think of how it could've been if she had.

Nadia drifted off to sleep with Mr. Sexy Ass on her mind, but she was awakened when Steve came through the door. Startled, she jumped up.

"Uh huh," he said. "You must've been dreaming of something wrong, by the way you jumped."

Nadia prayed she wasn't moaning or saying something in her sleep. She stared at him for a moment, half scared out of her mind, but Steve was smiling. That's when she realized he was carrying bags of groceries. He set them down and went out to the car to retrieve the rest. She escaped to the bathroom and washed her face. When she returned to the living room, Steve was still bringing in grocery bags.

"Baby, we gonna do it up for Malik and Karen this weekend," Steve said excitedly, as he put down the last bag. He walked by her, playfully smacked her on the butt and kissed her on the cheek.

Why in the hell is he so excited?

"I went to the gas station and filled up the tank for the grill."

"You're grilling for them?"

"Hell yeah. Maybe, if Karen has a good time here, it will carry over for them when they leave."

Wow, how kind of my husband to think of saving Malik's marriage by making sure Karen was happy. Mr. Lowe's words rang in her head. *"There's a whole lot behind a little bit."* Nadia walked into the kitchen and started unpacking the grocery bags. She was completely amazed. Chicken, shrimp, a slab of ribs, pasta, juices. What the hell? She was unsure if her feelings showed on her face, but she felt Steve's hands slowly wrap around her waist. She tensed up.

"Thank you so much, baby," he said softly in her ear.

"And what exactly are you thanking me for?" Nadia removed fresh broccoli from the bag, slipped away from his grasp and opened the refrigerator.

"I'm thanking you for that one hundred dollars that you had stashed away." He grabbed her around the waist and pulled her into him. "I wouldn't have been able to do this without your help." He kissed on the cheek and laughed.

He took my money! He took my money!

Yes, he took her money. The money her father had given her. The money she was going to use to spoil herself.

He went into my wallet, behind my cards and really took my money!

"I couldn't believe my luck when I found that money," he said turning her to face him. "I know that Malik has a sneaky bitch on his hands, but I didn't think that I did."

Nadia said not a word. She was angry and confused. Angry

because he took her money and confused because she felt a little better with him calling Karen a sneaky bitch.

"I wasn't trying to hide the money," she lied. "I guess I forgot that it was there." She wanted the conversation to end. The money was gone and she just had to deal with it.

"It doesn't matter because I found it." With that said, he walked out of the kitchen and into the living room. Surprisingly, Steve started cleaning up. She finished putting up the groceries and the extra things that Steve purchased, with the help of her money.

Tired, she went into the bedroom and sat down. Her mind was going a million miles per hour and she had to entertain company she really didn't want in her house. Lying back on the bed, and surprisingly, she fell into a deep sleep.

Two hours later, she woke to the hum of the vacuum cleaner. She walked into the living room to find Steve singing and vacuuming. She was dumbfounded, and couldn't believe her eyes. Steve had cleaned the living room, the dining room and the kitchen. She opened the bathroom door in the hallway and it was spotless.

"Hey, baby," he said, looking at her. "You can go ahead and lay back down. I got this. You're gonna need your energy to help cook tomorrow."

She didn't think twice. She went back into her room and closed the door. As she sat on the bed, Theresa rang her cell phone.

"Hey, Theresa. What's up girl?"

"Nothing, I was just calling to see how you were doing. I was thinking about everything that we talked about at work today and you looked distressed."

"Yeah, it was a little rough, but I know that y'all love me and wouldn't tell me anything wrong."

"So you're cool? You sound tired."

"I really am, but Steve just told me to come and get some rest."

Nadia purposely withheld information about the money and the groceries. She guessed, in her own way, she wanted Theresa to feel bad about what they said to her earlier. She secretly wanted Theresa to think she and Mr. Lowe were wrong about Steve.

"Well, that's a change in a positive direction. Miracles do happen," she said, followed with laughter.

Nadia chuckled. "Girl, let me go. I'm gonna take a bath and relax. Steve is cleaning up and I'm enjoying every bit of it."

"Whaaat? Yeah you better enjoy that! Whatever drug he's on you better make sure that he overdoses on it!" Theresa said, laughing. "Okay girl. Talk to you later."

The truth was she didn't feel all that happy. If Steve was doing all this cooking and cleaning for her, she would feel great. However, she knew none of it was for her. None of it.

Chapter 14

Surprisingly, Steve didn't bother Nadia for sex last night. That was strange, especially knowing she was off her cycle. She wasn't sure how to feel, but for some reason it felt like the calm before the storm.

Steve didn't sleep in the room last night, so Nadia guessed he was still out on the couch. It was a little after nine o'clock in the morning, which was late for Nadia. She wasn't one for sleeping in.

While brushing her teeth, she smelled something smoky. Curious, she made her way to the kitchen. Steve had the grill going.

"Getting started early, huh?" she asked him.

"Good morning, baby." He wore an apron and he looked good. He was clean-shaven and full of energy. "I wanted to get started early so that everything would be perfect when they got here."

"Well, I will help as soon as I get washed up."

"Hurry up, baby. We have a few more things to do before they get here. I talked to Malik and he said they would be here around three."

Again, that strange feeling tugged at Nadia's gut. Why couldn't Steve be like this for her? She did so much around the house, waiting on him hand and foot, ensuring he was comfortable and that his needs were met, yet she felt very much unappreciated. But now that his best friend and the sneaky bitch were coming over, all of a sudden, they were working as a team. Nadia was baffled, but she didn't complain. She was happy that she didn't have to clean the house for once.

There's a whole lot behind a little bit, she thought. "Shut up, Mr. Lowe," she said out loud, as she walked into the bathroom.

While washing her face, she realized that Steve still hadn't pestered her for sex. Although it was strange, she was going to enjoy it while it lasted.

෨ ෨ ෨

"Baby, could you steam these shrimp for me?" Steve asked sweetly, as she walked into the kitchen. Truly, this was the most she'd heard him calling her baby in years.

"Sure."

They cooked the entire morning. Steve was on the grill and she in the kitchen preparing most of the side dishes. They finished with the cooking very close to two o'clock.

"Hurry up and get yourself together," Steve said. "They'll be here soon and I want our shit to be together."

Nadia showered and slipped into a pair of jeans and a long sleeve, black, cross front shirt. After her usual grooming, she sat on the couch.

Twenty minutes later, she smelled Steve before she saw him. He was sharp as a tack, wearing jeans and a crisp, ironed, long sleeve dress shirt that she had never seen before. Nadia looked him up and down; he was wearing shoes she'd never seen before—dressy casual with the pointed toe.

"So how do I look?" Steve asked, posing for her.

"You look great." She tried to force a smile. Something in her spirit told her she was in for an interesting evening.

Malik and Karen were knocking on the door a little after three.

"Can you get that baby?" Steve said.

Although they both were sitting on the couch, why did she have to be the one to answer the door? She didn't bother to ask, she just did as she was told.

"Hello," said Karen's titties, which was all Nadia saw when she answered the door. She wore a top that was cut so low that if she turned the wrong way a nipple would pop out. Her lips were shining as if she smothered Crisco on them, and she had a long, feathery, brownish, blondish weave going on.

"Hey girl," she said, giving Nadia a hug.

Malik walked in behind her and gave Nadia a hug and a kiss on the cheek, but said nothing.

"*Steve*," Karen squealed and ran over to him as he sat on the couch. She sat down next to him and gave him a huge hug.

"What's up man?" Malik said, sitting next to Karen and pulling her in to him.

Nadia was the only one standing and she felt uncomfortable as hell in her own house.

"You look so cute," Karen said to Nadia. "Can you please take my coat for me?"

Karen seductively stood up, and took off her coat, exposing a tight, black shirt with a beaded necklace that stopped right at her cleavage and a pair of black leggings. Steve checked her out and Malik shifted uneasily.

Karen resumed her seat, and Nadia hung her coat in the closet. For a few moments, there was an awkward silence.

"It seems like I haven't seen the two of you in a long time. I know I haven't talked to either of y'all in a while. I was so happy when Malik told me that y'all had invited us over," Karen said a little too cheerfully for Nadia's taste.

Well, well, motherfucking well. Sneaky bitch really has no idea that my husband has talked to me about her, Nadia thought, as she moved into the living room.

"Yeah, Karen," Steve said in agreement. "It's been a while since I've talked to you. I talk to Malik all the time though and I'm always asking him about you."

Nadia stared at Steve in utter amazement, as he played into this lie. Had he forgotten that he told her everything?

"Awww, that's sweet of you to ask about me," Karen said, batting her eyes at Steve.

"So, Nadia, how you been doing?" Malik asked.

For a second, Nadia did not respond because she was still in shock over the game her husband was playing with his best friend right in her face.

"I'm good," she said. "Can I get you two something to drink?"

"We're okay for right now," Malik said.

Steve looked up at Nadia. "Well, could you please get me a soda?"

With a heavy heart and battling back tears, Nadia walked into the kitchen and grabbed a grape soda for Steve. She walked over to the couch and handed the soda to him. He popped it open, took a sip and then put it on the table.

"So, how have you two been doing?" Steve asked.

"We're good," Malik said. "Nothing out of the ordinary, you know how it is."

"Yeah, me and my baby are doing well, too," Steve said, looking at Nadia.

Karen's lips tightened.

"We've been cooking all day," Steve continued. "Y'all better eat up."

"Oh you know it's going down," Malik said, rubbing his stomach. "What y'all got grilling? You can smell that grilled food all the way outside."

"I just put on some ribs and chicken. It was cold out there, but I couldn't help myself. I had to do it up for y'all."

As Malik and Steve continued to make small talk, Steve's eyes kept darting from Malik to Karen's breasts, as if they were having their own conversation. Karen adjusted herself a little on the couch and then she reached over to the table, picked up the soda, took a sip and handed it to Steve. He continued talking with Malik as if nothing happened. Then he took a sip, put the soda back down on the table and kept talking.

Nadia was fucking livid. The bitch hadn't been there for five minutes and already she felt like an outsider in her own house. How was she comfortable enough with Nadia's husband to drink from his soda can?

Easy because your dumb ass just let it happen, said Nadia's conscience.

"Malik, let's go on outside on the patio and talk about some things. We can let these ladies talk since it's been a while for them."

Malik looked at Nadia, and she wasn't sure if he was waiting for her to say something about the soda, or maybe she was waiting for him to say something. Either way, they both said nothing, but their facial expressions spoke volumes.

Not wanting to be in Karen's presence, Nadia watched the guys leave the room and reluctantly moved toward the chair in the corner. She certainly wasn't going to sit beside the bitch, that's for sure.

"So, what you been up to?" Karen asked in the sweetest voice.

"Nothing much," Nadia said, trying to keep her composure. "You know…same old, same old. Work, work, and more work."

"I know what you mean. The last time I talked to Steve, he was telling me about how well the kids were doing in school and he said it was all because of you."

Listening intently, Nadia's eyes were glued to Karen, as she told her about everything that was going on in her house. From what her family had for dinner to silly things that Darryl and

Danielle had done to the time Steve gets off work and picks up Darryl, and so on.

Nadia felt like a pressure cooker, ready to explode. She was hot as hell. Had Karen forgotten that she just made a big production about how she hadn't talked to either of them? *Mental note.*

Steve walked back into the living room with Malik. "You pretty things ready to eat?"

"I'm starving," Karen said. "Let's eat up. Where can I wash my hands?"

"You know where the bathroom is," Steve said.

"Oh, yeah," Karen said.

"Let me check and make sure there's some soap in there for you," Steve said, walking into the bathroom with Karen trailing right behind him.

Karen's giggles were audible, but Nadia just couldn't bring herself to walk into the bathroom. Ditto for Malik, as both of their dumb asses just stood there and took that blatant disrespect for the second time today.

Steve returned and patted Malik on the back. "Let's eat!"

Admittedly, they did have a nice spread. All the food was sitting out on the counter top. Karen joined them, taking a seat at the table and every piece of titty she owned was on that table, as well.

Steve got a plate from the cabinet and began fixing it up with a variety of food. Malik grabbed a plate and did the same. Nadia watched as Steve acted like someone she didn't recognize.

While she liked seeing this domestic side of him, her thoughts and feelings were betraying her. She sat down at the table with Karen. When Steve finished fixing the plate, he walked over to the table and sat the plate in front of Karen.

"Thank you, *Steve*," she sang, putting emphasis on his name. "That's so sweet."

"I was fixing her plate, man," Malik said.

"Oh, my fault, bro," Steve said with utter sincerity in his voice. "I just figured guests should eat first. I was gonna make your plate, too."

That bullshit comment seemed to make Malik calm down a little.

"Alright, man, thanks," Malik said. "Nadia, here, you can just have this plate and I will get another one."

"Nah, I got Nadia's plate," Steve said. "You go ahead and eat that one."

Steve shot her a look as if she had just done something wrong. She felt like she was in trouble and she hadn't done a thing.

"You sure?" Malik said.

"Man, sit down," Steve said. "Eat and enjoy."

Malik took a seat beside his wife, and caressed her shoulders. Steve spotted it from the corner of his eye and, for a hot minute, a frown graced his face. He cleared his throat.

"Nadia, what do you want on your plate?" Steve asked.

Now he just fixed Karen's plate, I'm his wife, and he has to ask me what I want, Nadia thought. "To be honest with you, I'm not that hungry right now."

"Cool. Guess I'll fix my plate then."

Steve did just that and sat down at the table. Nadia sat at the table, too, and listened. Steve and Malik reminisced about things they had done when they were younger. They talked about old school friends and old girlfriends. They were laughing and joking and Nadia sat there on the verge of throwing up.

She felt the need to move, so she got up and started clearing away the dishes. "Malik if you're finished, I can take your plate."

Steve kept laughing, but shot her a look when she asked for Malik's plate. *The green-eyed monster, maybe?* Nadia quickly asked Karen the same, and took her plate and then Steve's plate. The three of them went back into the living room and Nadia was left to clean the kitchen.

Where was "Mr. We Gotta Have *Everything* Straight" now that this kitchen was a mess? Quite honestly, Nadia was relieved to have a break away from them. It gave her a chance to think on what was happening right in her face. The atmosphere just didn't feel right. It just felt like evil was floating throughout her home.

She took her sweet time cleaning up the kitchen and then joined them back in the living room. Nadia and Steve sat opposite of Malik and Karen, who were sitting on the other couch across from them. Will Downing was playing in the background. It was now a little after six and the sun had set.

"I'll be right back," Steve said. He returned a few seconds later with a candle from their bedroom and matches. He lit the candle, put it on the table and then turned off the lights.

The flickering light from the candle set the mood to sexy and uncomfortable. Steve resumed his seat next to his wife and caressed her thigh.

Karen's eyes were glued on Steve. As Nadia watched Karen watching Steve, she noticed that Karen's titties seemed to be glistening from the candlelight. That's when Nadia realized that Steve had the best seat in the house. *These motherfuckers are romancing each other right in front of Malik and I.*

"I can't wait 'til later," Steve said, turning his attention toward Nadia.

"Why is that?" Malik said.

"I'm ready to make love to my lady," he said, rubbing his hand up and down her thigh. Karen was enticed by Steve's affection toward Nadia.

"Damn man, that's what I'm talking about. You hear that Karen?"

"I heard it, baby," she said, looking at Malik with lust in her eyes. "You want this later?"

"I wish I could get it now," Malik said, looking into Karen's eyes.

Karen leaned in and kissed Malik. The kiss was explosive. She kissed him slowly, her tongue moving in and out of his mouth with slow precision. Then Karen began massaging her own breast, never letting her lips leave Malik's. Nadia looked at Steve. This nigga was in a daze and she clearly saw his dick sitting on his thigh. Then, as if they remembered where they were, they stopped.

"I'm sorry," Malik said, beaming with satisfaction. "My baby even caught me off guard with that."

Malik had a boner, too, and Nadia, too, had the perfect seat in the house. The sexual tension in the air was high and the mood was right for naughty conversation. A conversation that she preferred not to partake in, as it was not her cup of tea.

"We're all grown," Steve started. "Right?"

"Yeah," Karen and Malik said in unison.

Nadia nodded and wondered where the hell this was going.

"So we're not taking anything serious here, but let's just talk about a few what ifs."

"Okay," everyone said again.

"Has anyone here ever thought about having a threesome?" Steve asked.

Nadia blinked her eyes, as she couldn't believe her ears. Her heart began to race and she instantly felt clammy all over.

"Well," said Karen, "I can honestly say I've thought about it, but I've never done it."

"Me, too," Malik added. "Karen and I have discussed threesomes, but just in general, not doing it for real."

Steve looked at me. "What about you, babe?"

"Uh, no, I've never thought about that."

Steve looked disgusted. "Baby, you need to lighten up. Look at how Malik and Karen can talk about these things and you and I never talk about stuff like this. Malik, it must be nice to have a cool ass wife to talk to."

Karen looked at Nadia and asked, "Are you serious?" adding fuel to the fire. Karen looked down at her own breasts and began slowly massaging around her nipples through the outside of her shirt. Then she slowly opened her legs. "I think I could handle another woman sucking on these babies while I'm getting fucked."

I swear that woman has a dick or she has the biggest pussy I've ever seen in my life, Nadia thought, as she could see the total outline of her lips through her leggings. And, she noted, Steve's dick saw it, too.

"That's what I'm talking about," Steve said. "Malik, you one lucky dude. Nadia, you need to get with that shit."

Nadia was dumbfounded. She simply could not believe that Malik didn't have a problem with his wife acting like a porn star. Or, maybe he thought it was sexy for his wife to act in that way.

"Well," Steve probed further. "What about anal sex?"

Okay, this is too much, she thought, shaking her head, as this conversation was about to make her sick.

Malik and Karen looked at each other and started smiling.

"You're right, we are grown," Malik said, pulling Karen close to him. "I hit that ass at least once a week."

Karen was grinning from ear to ear. "There's nothing I won't do for my man," she said, eyeing Steve with sexual intensity. "Nothing."

"That's the shit I want," Steve said, sitting so that his erection was noticeable to everyone. He looked at Nadia and she looked away.

Steve had asked her about anal sex before and she told him she would never do such a thing. She had a rough pregnancy with Darryl and as she was delivering, she pushed so hard that she developed hemorrhoids. They hurt so badly and she knew that she wouldn't be able to handle anything anally.

"So you gonna give me that ass or what, Nadia?" Steve asked.

Knowing about her hemorrhoids, why would he put her on the spot like that in front of Malik and Karen?

"Steve, can we talk about this later?" She tried to sound sensual instead of uncomfortable.

"See what I'm saying?" Steve said. "She claims she can't do it for some reason, but I'm coming for that ass."

"Come on, Nadia," Karen chimed in. "The orgasm is amazing and if it makes your man feel good you better get with it. I learned that what a wife won't do another woman will. That's why I make sure my man gets what he wants."

"Damn, how often you get that pussy?" Steve asked Malik.

Was this normal? Did anyone see the disrespect in this conversation or was Nadia just being a sour puss?

"At least three or four times a week. My baby lays it down for me."

Nadia looked at Steve, and she had never seen a dick deflate so quickly in her life. She sat up.

"Is that right?" Steve said, looking a little upset.

"That's why I don't trip off of any other women. Why would I have to? I get everything I need at home."

Karen closed her legs some, which brought on icy stares.

Steve suddenly turned toward Nadia. "Shit, man. I get it damn near every night, too."

Steve got really close to Nadia and pressed his lips against hers, kissing her passionately as he gently massaged her breast. He moved his lips down to her neck, as his finger circled her nipple.

That's all it took for Malik and Karen to start up, again. Malik took it to another level and began massaging Karen's pussy through her clothes, as she softly moaned. Steve started kissing Nadia on the lips and he began to moan. Malik began to massage Karen's clitoris a little faster as he continued kissing her. Steve put his hand inside Nadia's shirt, massaging her bare nipple. Karen moaned, Steve moaned.

"Oh shit," Karen exclaimed. "Malik, we better stop before we end up fucking on this couch."

"You're right, babe," Malik said.

But Steve didn't stop. He had an audience now. Steve kissed down Nadia's neck to her breast and stuck his tongue inside of her shirt. Flicking her nipple with his tongue, he began to massage between her thighs.

"Steve," Nadia said. "They're watching us."

"Damn, baby," he said. "That shit was getting good to me. Guess we better stop."

Nadia was so embarrassed. *Why did I just let him exploit me like that?*

Immediately, Karen's whole attitude seemed to change. She got up and went to the closet. "Let's go baby," she said.

"Oh, you ready to go home to daddy, huh?" Malik said, standing up.

Karen didn't answer. She just put on her coat, opened the door and went outside.

"Guess the night's over then," Malik said, grabbing his jacket and heading for the door. "Mommy's hot for Daddy right now. Gotta go handle my business. I'll call you tomorrow, man," he said to Steve, and headed out the door.

Steve stared at the door for a few moments and then turned his attention back to Nadia. He was ready and she was in for it.

He pushed her back on the couch and climbed on top of her, slowly grinding. Nadia could feel his erection poking her. He put his hands underneath her butt and lifted her into him. He was kissing her neck with such sensuality she almost enjoyed it. He moved his mouth up to her ear.

"Did you see Karen's titties?"

Did I just hear my husband right?

"Did you see how nice and round they were? Her nipples are probably big and brown and pretty as shit."

Nadia was stunned.

"Mmmmm, I bet her nipples taste so good," he said, moaning in her ear.

Steve stood up, unzipped his pants, and pulled out his dick, pointing it at her mouth. "Karen, suck this dick," he said.

Nadia looked at her husband; his eyes were somewhere else. She opened her mouth and took him in.

"Yeah, Karen, Daddy's dick taste good, don't it?"

Steve humped her mouth, but was surprisingly gentle. Probably, she thought, because he was mentally fucking Karen.

Steve withdrew his dick from the warmth of her mouth and helped her out of her shirt. He sucked her nipples, moaning and groaning. "Mmmm, they taste so good." He moved from one to the other before coming back up and tongue kissing his wife. Somehow, he got her pants and underwear off. He moved on her slowly as he pushed himself inside of her. "Damn, Karen. Your pussy is so tight."

Steve made love to Nadia in such a way that all she wanted to do was cry. Because, he wasn't making love to her, but to another woman. His dick even felt different inside of her. He was harder than she'd ever known him to be and it wasn't even for her.

Steve stroked faster. "Karen, this pussy is so good. You're gonna make me cum. Make me cum, Karen. Cum on my dick, Karen. Karen, Karen, shit, Karen, I'm cumming!"

Steve pulled out of her and jacked all over her, squirting on her stomach, her face, in her hair and on the couch. She couldn't look at him. Instead, she just laid there with closed eyes and waited for him to finish.

Once the thrill was gone, Steve looked down at her melancholy face. "What's wrong, baby?" Steve asked.

Tears streamed from her eyes.

"We were just role playing," he said. "It was nothing personal. I thought you were grown up enough to handle stuff like that."

She remained silent, allowing her tears to flow.

"You've got to be kidding me," Steve said, as he got up. "You're seriously crying over something as silly as that? I was just trying to spice up our lovemaking." Steve stood beside the couch with still a very noticeable erection. "Look, when you grow the fuck up let me know," he said, shaking his head and walking toward the bedroom.

Nadia was at an all-time low. She was broken. She stayed on the couch all night with remnants of dry cum all over her. She couldn't move.

She just wanted to lay there and die.

Chapter 15

The door slammed. That's how she woke up on Sunday morning. Steve left her there butt naked on the couch and he was gone, without a clue as to where he was going. And, she didn't give a shit either.

Sitting up, a powerful wave of the previous night's events crashed down on her. Her house felt like a den of iniquity; a black cloud hung over her and it wouldn't leave her alone. Standing, she couldn't make it to her room without collapsing to the floor. She cried hysterically from a place that she didn't know was within her. Feeling the carpet against her skin, she curled up into a ball and let it all out.

"Jesus. Jesus!"

Before she knew it, she was screaming at the top of her lungs. She jumped up and started pounding the walls.

"Jesus!"

A burst of energy shot through her. "Jesus, help me!" She dropped to the floor and into the fetal position again.

Calming a little, she rocked her naked, cum-stained body back and forth. Nadia was like a mad woman for a few minutes, and now she was tired, but she managed to get up. She ran a hot bath, soaked for a while and replayed the previous night's events.

"My husband made love to another woman last night with my body. And I *let* him do it," she sobbed. "Mr. Lowe told me that I let him get away with too much and now this *was* over the top. How could I ever tell anyone that my husband had sex with someone else through me?" The thought made her cry all over again. Nadia never thought that she would hit an all-time low like that. What the hell was wrong with her?

She sat in the tub for about an hour. She felt numb. Was this it? Was this her life?

ɔ ɔ ɔ

Nadia didn't have the energy for church, so she climbed into bed and stared at the ceiling instead. She felt heavy and she cried for hours, occasionally looking out the window. It was a cloudy day. Perfect for her mood.

Knowing she hadn't eaten in twenty-four hours, she simply wasn't hungry. The thought of food made her stomach and head ache. She was now feeling something she'd never felt before. Depression.

Her life was fucked up. *How could he do that to me?* she asked herself repeatedly, as she pulled the covers up over her head. She simply did not want to live anymore.

What was the point? Life hurts too much. Steve knew of her issues with molestation, and he used it against her. He knew her weakness and figured he could play that vulnerability to his advantage. How could a husband do that to his wife? How could he say another woman's name while making love to the woman he vowed to love, honor and protect, through sickness and health, 'til death do them part?

Nadia curled up tighter into a ball, as her stomach felt like it was embarking on a one-hundred-foot roller coaster drop. How could she let him do that? Why didn't she speak up?

He doesn't love me. Hell, I don't love me.

Her phone rang a few times. It was her father, but she didn't answer it. At that moment, she didn't care about anything anymore. She pulled her knees in to her chest and buried herself under the blanket where she planned to hibernate for as long as it took the pain to subside. For some reason, she felt better shutting out the world, alone in her darkness where she felt safe from all harm, and from Steve.

Several hours had passed, and Nadia was awakened by the phone. It was her father. This time, she chose to answer it.

"Hello."

"Baby, what's wrong? Why do you sound like that?"

"I'm just sleeping, Daddy. I think I'm coming down with something."

"I was wondering why I hadn't heard from you. Do you just want me to keep the kids and take them to school tomorrow? I can check to see how you're feeling and if you're still not feeling well then I can keep them until you get your strength back up."

"Yes, Daddy. Please keep them tonight. I don't want them to catch whatever it is I'm coming down with." Nadia felt awful lying to her daddy, but she could hardly get up to go to the bathroom, let alone drive to pick up her children.

"Go to sleep and feel better, baby. Talk to you later."

"Thank you, Daddy. Bye."

Nadia turned off her cell phone, curled up and retreated to her safety zone under the darkness of her blanket.

∽ ∽ ∽

"What the hell is wrong with you?" Steve asked, snatching the blankets off her. "It's almost seven-thirty and you're in here sleeping. You haven't done shit in this house since I've been gone."

"I don't feel good," she managed to utter.

"Another excuse not to fuck, huh?" Steve threw the blanket back on her. "Where are the kids?"

"Ma and Daddy are keeping them because I don't feel well," she said from under the blanket.

"Yeah right," he said and walked out of the room.

She curled up.

Steve actually did her a favor by throwing that blanket on her. It covered her completely, shutting him out of her lonely world. She was in the comfort of her darkness. Nothing else seemed to love her, but the darkness definitely did.

Chapter 16

The next morning, Nadia called in sick. The sun was shining and she was angry. She needed another cloudy day. The sun meant that life still went on. So, she shut it out. She closed the blinds and made her room as dark as possible. Life was stopping in this room as far as she was concerned. Somehow, the sun still managed to creep in.

Steve walked into the room. "Guess you're not going to work. Well, I'll see you when I get home. Let me know if you need anything."

She didn't answer. Moments later, the door closed.

It seemed that no matter how hard she tried glimpses of sunlight kept peeking through. The darkness under the blankets wasn't even the same. The sun was positioned with the rays pointing directly at the bed.

"Okay, okay, you win," she said and sat up.

Nadia walked into the kitchen, got a piece of bread out and tried to eat it, but she could only take a bite. Her appetite was completely gone. She hadn't eaten anything in two days.

The phone rang. It was Theresa. Nadia didn't answer. There was no way Nadia could tell her what happened and somehow Nadia figured that if Theresa heard her voice, she would know it all.

Nadia sat out on the couch. The thoughts of that night hit her again, but she had no more tears. She was just filled with shame. She didn't even know how to go to God on this. She couldn't find the words to pray. She was mentally drained. All she could do was call His name and hope He would handle the rest.

Nadia turned on the television and lay in a zombie like state for the entire day. Everything about her life just hurt and she wasn't sure how to deal with it. There wasn't a woman on the face of the Earth that would allow her husband to call out another woman's name in bed. He didn't even respect her enough to keep his thoughts to himself while he was fucking her.

Nadia watched a few shows on television and the day zoomed by. She decided that maybe she should shower. Walking in the bathroom, she turned on the water to let it warm up. She went to the sink and realized that she couldn't even look at herself in the mirror. She was completely ashamed of herself. She forced herself to look in the mirror and she was horrified. Had she aged in two days? She had a few gray hairs that she knew weren't there two days ago. Nadia had bags under her eyes although she slept the whole day yesterday. And she knew she dropped at least five pounds, something she couldn't afford to do with her already small frame.

The steam started coming from the shower and Nadia undressed and stepped in under the streaming water. She stood under the water, hair and all and let it pelt away at her diminishing body. She knew that she was mentally affected by the abuse that Steve inflicted on her. But now it was affecting her physically. She didn't even have the energy to wash. She must've stayed under the water for at least twenty minutes before she just turned it off. She got out, dried off, put back on the same pajamas and got back in the bed. She got in her comfortable fetal position, pulled the blankets over her and slept for the next three hours.

The phone woke her up. It was Steve.

"Hello."

"What's for dinner? Wait, are you sleeping? Have you been sleeping all day?"

"I told you that I didn't feel good, Steve."

"You couldn't manage to get up to fix a little dinner?"

"I'm getting up, Steve."

He hung up.

Nadia managed to throw together chicken Alfredo and broccoli. And she did it with no love. She decided that she was going to go to work the next day. Staying home made her feel worse, but she didn't want anyone on the outside to see her. She needed help. She called her doctor and made an appointment. She needed a pill or something to help her. She saw commercials for depression all of the time. She wanted to deny what was happening to her, but she needed this heaviness to go away.

Nadia was able to get an appointment for twelve noon the next day. That meant that she would just take a half day from work. She didn't want Steve to know that she was going. There were some truths that she had to get ready to face, and his interference was the last thing she needed.

A few hours later, Steve came through the door. The sight of him literally made her sick. He may have been a good-looking man to people on the outside, but he was ugly as hell to her, inside and out.

"Damn," he said, closing the door behind him. "What's wrong with your head? Did you and your comb have a fight or something?"

Nadia didn't answer him.

He continued. "Who wants to come home to a woman looking like that? You know what, I'm gonna step out and grab something. I can't be sitting in here with you looking all fucked up."

And just like that, he turned around and was gone.

He couldn't even see what he was doing to her. She was deteriorating and he was looking healthy as shit. She couldn't wash and he smelled like cologne. She couldn't comb her hair and he could shave his head. She had on the same clothes and he was dressed to kill. She couldn't eat and he just went out to eat.

Nadia left the food on the stove and returned to her darkness. Once again, she curled up, protecting herself in the fetal position, and began rocking. Rocking and crying.

God, I need You, she said to herself. *Because I don't want to wake up in the morning.*

Chapter 17

The next day, Nadia pulled herself up off the bed and took a shower. She was able to wash, and go about her usual routine, but it took every ounce of energy she had. She called her father and told him she wasn't feeling well, and that she was staying home. Nadia needed time to herself.

Steve was gone. *Thank God*, she thought, as she looked at the food still on the stove from the previous night. She threw her hand in the air, waving off any notion of her cleaning up the mess.

Grabbing her purse and keys, she dragged herself out the front door and stood on the front porch, with her face pointed up toward the warm sun. It felt good on her face. She inhaled deeply, trying to muster up the energy to do anything. Reluctantly, she put one foot in front of the other, and made it to her car. Once inside, she gripped the steering wheel and held on tight. She felt exhausted, like she'd run a marathon. It took everything for her not to cancel her appointment and revert to her darkness.

Walking into the primary care physician's office somehow made her feel better, and she was the only one in the waiting area. After checking in, Nadia sat down and began to cry. Shocked by her tears, as she was so exhausted, she had no idea where they came from. Maybe it was because she knew she was losing her mind and this was a battle she was going to have to fight on her own. She prayed that she would find the relief she needed in a pill.

"Nadia Stevenson, please come back."

Nadia followed Dr. Middleton into the patient room. "So, how can I help you today?" Dr. Middleton asked. She was a short, white woman who looked a little too cheerful for Nadia today.

"Well, I think I might be depressed."

"Why do you think that?" Dr. Middleton jotted down notes.

Nadia explained what had happened over the past two days.

"Well we normally wait to see if what is happening to you goes on for two weeks or more, but it definitely does sound like depression. And you haven't eaten?"

"No."

"I know that it will be difficult, but you have to eat something. You will feel a little better. Eating nothing only helps you to feel worse in your depressed state."

Nadia nodded, but she did not intend to force herself to eat. Was she somehow punishing herself by denying herself food? Was she abusing herself?

"Well let's see how we can help you," Dr. Middleton said.

Nadia didn't know what to expect or how doctors determined how to prescribe which pill, but she did know that she needed something.

"So, let's see," she said, looking through a rather extensive list. "Let's start you out on Wellbutrin for a few weeks. You let me know how this is working for you and if you don't like it we can change it up until you find what you like."

What the fuck am I? A lab rat!

"There's no sort of test or something that I can take to help determine which pill is best for me?"

Dr. Middleton shook her head. "I'm afraid not. I will just have to prescribe different pills for you until you find one that you like. I will tell you though that there are definitely side effects. You may experience insomnia, some hallucinating and a loss of libido. And, in some cases, the depression gets worse first before the medicine really kicks in and makes you feel better."

"So, I could start taking the medicine and my depression will get more depressing?"

"Yes, but you will start to feel better in a week or two if that's the right pill for you."

"And if it's not?"

"Then you can make an appointment and we can try something else." Dr. Middleton's attitude was the norm; nonchalant and almost uncaring since she dealt with cases like Nadia's every day. "There's another thing," Dr. Middleton continued. "If you decide that you want to come off of a pill you can't just stop cold turkey. You have to break down the dosage and slowly wean yourself off of the pill. If you just stop taking it your depression could come back two times worse than it was."

"Okay, let me get this straight. If the pill that you prescribe isn't the pill for me, I can't just stop taking it. I have to wean myself off of the pill that's not for me and try a new pill that could potentially not be for me either?"

"To be honest, I've never heard it put like that before, but unfortunately to answer your question, yes. That is exactly what I'm saying."

Well, damn, Nadia thought, and said nothing for a moment. Nadia felt she needed something, but would she be making matters worse? Once again, she felt defeated. She thought she would be able to take a miracle in a pill and her problems would disappear.

"So, should I prescribe the Wellbutrin for you, Ms. Stevenson?"

Nadia thought about it. "No thank you. I will just have to figure something else out."

"Well, if you change your mind, just come back to see me."

"I will, but I don't think I will be changing my mind. Thank you so much, Dr. Middleton."

Nadia left the doctor's office feeling a little stronger than when she walked in. The sun was shining and she realized she had made a decision that was a good one for her. She turned the radio to the gospel station and drove to the grocery store.

"God is all I need, God is all I need," came from the radio.

"I hear you Lord. You're all I need."

❧ ❧ ❧

At the grocery store, Nadia shopped for the basics—bread, milk, water and eggs. She just couldn't bring herself to look for anything else. Nadia grabbed those items and went to the counter.

"Good evening," said the cashier. "Your total will be ten dollars and eighty cents."

Nadia took her debit card out of her purse and handed it to him. *He took my money my father gave to me*, Nadia thought as she waited for the cashier to run her card.

"I'm sorry, ma'am, but your card has been declined. Do you have another form of payment?"

"There must be a mistake," Nadia said. She was paid the previous Friday and she knew that she had ten dollars and eighty cents in her account.

"Let me try punching in the numbers on your card," said the cashier.

Nadia was beyond embarrassed, with a small line forming behind her.

"I'm so sorry, but your card is still declined."

Nadia took her card and walked out of the store. She couldn't take any more, as she sat in her car and fought back tears. It was no time to cry. She had to call her bank to see why her card was declined. Nadia went through all of the annoying bank prompts until she finally reached a live person.

"Your account number please." Nadia recited her account number. "How may I help you?"

"I just went to the grocery store to make a purchase for ten dollars and some change and my card was declined. I don't understand what the problem is."

"Let me check your account for you."

Nadia waited through seconds of silence.

"Well, Ms. Stevenson, you had a few bill pay payments go through."

"Okay, I know about those. So, there should still be money in my account."

"You also had a debit of one thousand forty dollars come through from a payday loan place."

"What do you mean?"

"All I can tell you is what I'm seeing on your account, Ms. Stevenson."

"So what is my account balance?"

"Negative two hundred twenty-three dollars and six cents."

"Negative!" Nadia screamed. "Negative! I didn't make any payday loan. Someone must've hacked into my account or something!"

"I'm sorry, Ms. Stevenson. If you want us to investigate this debit you can go online, fill out the necessary paperwork and we can begin looking into this."

"But what do I do in the meantime? I don't get paid for another two weeks!"

"I'm sorry. That's all I can do?"

Nadia hung up. Her head was spinning. Panic reverberated through her. Her money was gone...payday loan...what the fuck was going on?

Nadia looked on her phone and noticed her message light flashing. The first message was from her father telling her that he would keep the kids again. Great. Nadia listened to the second message.

> *"Good evening, this message is for Ms. Nadia Stevenson. You have failed to make payments on the two hundred dollars that you borrowed from us over the past three months. We have tried unsuccessfully to reach you. The total due on this loan, including interest and late fees, is one thousand forty dollars. The payment will be debited in the full amount this Friday. Thank you and have a good day."*

"What the fuck?" Nadia shouted. Nadia dialed the number. "Hello, we pay to make your day. How may I help you?"

"This is Nadia Stevenson. I just received a message saying that I owe a total of one thousand forty dollars. There must be some sort of mistake. I have never borrowed any money from you all."

"Ms. Stevenson, if you don't mind, please let me take a look at your account." The representative placed her on a five-minute hold. Her mind raced to all of the possibilities about what could've happened. "Ms. Stevenson, you took out a loan with us approximately three months ago for two hundred dollars. I am looking at the paper work."

"I didn't take out any loan. I don't even know where you all are located." Nadia began to cry into the phone.

"Ms. Stevenson, please don't cry. Let me look deeper into this. Perhaps there was some sort of mistake made. If need be, we may have to look into some sort of fraud on your account. Is it okay if I delve a little deeper and call you when I find out more?"

"Sure. And thank you for your help."

Nadia hung up and immediately called Steve. "Steve, somebody took out a loan in my name and…"

"Oh that was me," he said. "Damn, baby, I forgot all about that. I'm so sorry."

Nadia felt faint. It was too much. "Why did you take out a loan in my name?"

"I wanted to do something nice for you and the kids, but other stuff came up and I wasn't able to."

"Well, they're about to do an investigation into this loan."

"Just call them and tell them they don't have to do that."

"Steve, you took out a loan for two hundred dollars in my name that turned into one thousand forty!" Nadia yelled. "My account is in the negative because they took it out of my account."

"Calm the fuck down," Steve said in a low tone. Nadia guessed he couldn't get too loud in the restaurant where he worked. "I'll give you back your silly ass money. I just forgot that's all. Now call them and leave me alone about this shit." He hung up.

Nadia reluctantly did as she was told. She called the payday loan company back and told them it was all a big misunderstanding, but she did appreciate their willingness to help her. Nadia knew good and damn well that she wasn't going to get that money back.

Chapter 18

Nadia drove the long way home in complete silence. No radio. No nothing. What normally would have taken her thirty minutes took her close to two hours, putting her right around the time she would have been home from work. The maintenance light came on, letting her know she needed an oil change. How was she going to do that? Her head started pounding. By the time she got home, Steve was already there yet he wasn't supposed to get off of work for another few hours. Reluctant to go inside her own home, she sat in her car. She hated him and she hated that house. It wasn't a home. She loved her kids. However, Nadia realized there was no way Steve could love her.

She dragged herself out of the car and into the house. Steve had a beautiful bouquet of flowers on the table for her and he was in the kitchen marinating chicken breasts.

"Hey baby!" He walked over to her, grabbed her hand and led her to the couch. "I'm sorry about the money, boo," he said. "I really did forget about it. I just wanted to do something for you and I forgot. Then I had to get a few things done to my car and it just slipped my mind." He leaned in and kissed her on the cheek.

She simply stared at him. *I wondered if I should've just gotten the damn pills from the doctor.*

Again, taking her by the hand, he led her to the bathroom. Candles adorned the sink and on the side of the tub. A nice bubble bath was drawn for her with rose petals floating on top of the water, and a bath pillow. Her favorite smooth jazz CD played, topping off the perfect ambience.

Nadia was speechless.

"I just want you to relax baby," he said. "Let me take care of you tonight."

Admittedly, this felt better than the pain that she was experiencing. Looking at him, she wanted this to be how her man treated her all the time, but deep down she knew it was a deflection from him fucking up her money. Nadia lacked the energy to argue or even think about her life right now. She just wanted to relax her pains away.

"I'll be back to check on you," Steve said, closing the bathroom door behind him.

She closed her eyes, but every mental picture was something painful. Her body ached from her mental pain. She slept all the time. And, she had no clue on how to live the rest of her life. Maybe this was the beginning of God answering her prayers. Perhaps all the turmoil in her life was really a blessing, which finally led them to this point of appreciating each other. Today, at this very moment, Steve was doing something for her. And, it felt good. She knew that God has His own way of working things out and maybe, just maybe, things were getting ready to change for them.

That thought allowed her to relax a little more. Although she was still bothered by the fact that she was broke, he did tell her that he would give her back the money. This was his chance to show her how much he loved her and she so badly wanted him to love her. She wanted her family.

Steve returned to the bathroom and kneeled by the tub. He had a bath sponge in his hand. He dipped it into the water, lathered it with soap and bathed her. No words were spoken. He didn't even try anything kinky. *Well, what do you know?* This really was about her.

When he was finished bathing her, he helped her out of the tub. He got the baby oil and rubbed it all over her body.

"Don't move," he said.

Steve went to her drawer and pulled out a nightgown. He dressed her and walked her to the bed. He pulled back the covers, helped her in, handed her the remote and walked back out to the kitchen.

Nadia flipped through the channels, but she couldn't find anything she wanted to watch. She simply wanted to revel in this bittersweet moment. The inspiration to write was upon her, so she fetched her notebook. She felt herself pushing down her pain every time it tried to surface. She could write about a million things, but one issue particularly pressed on her mind. Karen. She had to get it out. She flipped the notebook to a blank page and began to write.

Her

On nights like this, oh what bliss
I love your kiss
I hold you, I touch you
A lifetime of happiness, my wife, my life

We make passionate love
I love you, I lick you
I can't wait to get in you
Your body is mines, my mind is not yours

You see, I see Her face
It's Her I want to taste
But you receive the pleasures
That I want to give to someone else

I'm penetrating you, but I'm feeling Her
My desire is on fire for Her touch
I hear you moan, but it's not your tone
It's Her mouth that I feel when I'm being blown

Damn I love you my beautiful wife
My mind is filled with lustful intentions, not to mention
Her, who I make love to when I'm with you
Does my body tell, can you feel the lie?

You ride me, but I throb inside of you for Her
My body reacts as I feel Her insides inside of you
We are as one, but it's Her that makes me cum
Now we're through and you have no clue

My beautiful wife, I thank you.

Nadia amazed herself with some of the stuff she wrote. She re-read her poem and sadness engulfed her. How many times had her husband made love to Her with her? She shook off the thought, as it was now safely written down in her notebook, and tucked back in its special place. She climbed into bed and resumed the fetal position. Something about that position and being covered up made her feel safe. Before she knew it, she returned to the darkness and fell asleep.

"Baby, wake up," Steve said, standing over her with a dinner tray.

Nadia opened her eyes and sat up in the bed. He sat the tray down and propped a pillow behind her back, then placed the tray over her legs. He prepared grilled chicken breasts, baked potatoes, salad, dinner rolls and juice. He had a fresh, red rose laying on the tray and a note on a napkin that said, "I love you."

Nadia's appetite returned with a vengeance.

She smiled at him as he leaned in to kiss her. She couldn't stop the tears. Maybe her suffering really wasn't in vain. Steve walked out and returned a few moments later with his plate and joined her on the bed. For the first time in a long time, they talked. Not about anything going on with them, of course. But, they talked about the stories on the news and how there's been a rash of senseless murders on school campuses.

For the first time in a few days, she didn't feel that heaviness. Was her happiness wrapped up in her husband?

"Steve, when I was coming home, my maintenance light came on."

"I will take it to have it serviced in the morning. You just take my car."

You have got to be kidding me. Life was getting better by the minute.

"Oh, I meant to talk to you about something," Steve said.

"What's that?" She sipped her juice.

"I wanted to talk to you about how you disrespected me the other night."

"Huh? What are you talking about?" She felt that heaviness slowly creeping in again. This emotional roller coaster was exhausting.

"When Malik and Karen were here, you cleaned up Malik's plate first. I'm not gonna fuss too much about it, but I'm letting you know that my woman never puts another man in front of me, especially at my dinner table."

Is he serious?

"You got it?"

"I got it," she said.

Steve resumed talking about the next news story, which was about the constant battle that President Obama was having with the Republican Party.

When they finished eating, Steve took their plates to the kitchen. He took a shower, put on some clean under clothes and climbed into bed with Nadia. Steve pulled her close to him and held her. Her body was tense waiting for the touching and feeling. Nothing. Before she knew it, she heard him snoring softly. She couldn't believe it. She inhaled his fresh scent and remembered how it used to be. How could a person hate and love someone so much and at the same time?

After a few minutes, she sank back into her husband. She was going to work tomorrow. She needed to catch up on some things and she could feel God moving in her life and in her marriage.

Thank you, Lord. *Thank you.*

Chapter 19

The next morning, Nadia woke up before Steve. After breakfast, she showered, curled her hair and decided to wear something cute today. She was feeling good. Steve was still snoring and she wasn't going to wake him.

I love him, I love him, I love him.

She grabbed her purse and keys and headed out the door. It wasn't until she was half-way down the street that she remembered that Steve was going to take her car today.

Oh well, she thought. *I don't feel like going back in the house and getting his keys, so he can do it another day.*

At work, she made no effort of avoiding Theresa and Mr. Lowe. It was time for lunch, and they were coming into the library.

"Well hello, stranger," Theresa said, giving her a hug.

"Hey, baby," Mr. Lowe said. "Where in the hell have you been?"

"I was just feeling under the weather," she sort of lied. She had been feeling miserable lately.

"You do look like you've lost a few pounds," Theresa said, which almost pushed Nadia back into a state of sadness, but she fought it.

Mr. Lowe was staring her right in the face. "So, how are things otherwise?" he asked.

Nadia told them about what Steve did for her last night. However, she conveniently left out the details about the events that sent her into a depressive downfall. Mr. Lowe's words were in her head. There was definitely a whole lot more to the little bit that she was telling them.

"Well, the past couple of things that you've told us have been pretty positive," Theresa said, smiling and giving Nadia five.

"Thank you, girl." Nadia hugged her.

Mr. Lowe stared at her as if he was looking right through her façade. "I'm here if you need me," he said and left the library.

"What's with him?" Nadia asked.

"I don't know," Theresa said. "Maybe he's having a bad day."

When lunch was over and Theresa went back to her classroom, Nadia checked her cell phone. She had a text from Steve that read: *I love you.*

Life was good and getting better. She listened to the message left by her father, telling her that he would keep the kids for the week. *Yes!* The rest of her workday was great. Nadia was talking and laughing and she felt brand new.

For the first time in ages, Nadia was excited about going home. On the way, she was singing her heart out and loving life. Inside the house, there were no signs of Steve. She walked into the kitchen, washed her hands and started preparing a spaghetti dinner. As she was making the salad, Steve came through the door, smiling from ear to ear as he kissed her.

"Smells delicious," he said.

"Why thank you."

"Karen told me to thank you for a great time on Saturday."

Nadia paused and her heart sank.

He took the cooking spoon and tasted the sauce. "Excellent," he said and then went into the bedroom.

Her eyes watered. She was thrown back just that quickly. *Why do I feel like I am sharing my husband with his best friend's wife?* Nadia tried to have an open mind about it all, but it was constantly nagging at her. *"Let it go,"* she told herself.

The urge to talk hit her, so she walked into the bedroom toward the bathroom, and Steve was lying across the bed, butt naked with his dick in his hand.

"You know what I want, right?" he said, stroking himself.

"What?" she asked, feeling enveloped by a tidal wave of negative emotion.

"I want that ass."

"Steve, I don't think I can do that. What about my hemorrhoids?"

"But what about all I've done for you lately? Damn, baby, for once why can't you just be the wife that I need you to be? A little hurt won't kill you and it will make me so happy."

She sat on the edge of the bed. She could take it. And, things were getting better. She couldn't let them go back to the way they were.

"And, I know this is off the topic, but I will take your car in tomorrow."

"Okay," she said not really giving a damn about the car at that moment.

Steve sat up behind her and started kissing her earlobe. She was tense as hell. "Can you do this for me?" he whispered. "Nadia, can you give Daddy what he wants?"

"Yes," Nadia said. "I can take it for you."

"That's my girl."

Nadia was scared as hell and trying to tell herself that it wouldn't be that bad. Steve damn near ripped her clothes off and flipped her on her stomach, as he stood at the edge of the bed. He wet his fingers and massaged her rectum.

"I'm going in slowly now," he said.

"Okay." Nadia braced herself, as she felt Steve's body on top of hers.

Steve only put a piece of the tip in and she jumped across the bed. That little bit hurt like hell.

"Steve, I don't think I can do this," she pleaded.

"But you just said you would do it for me," he said softly, as grabbed her hips, and positioned Nadia on her stomach.

Steve went in again and when she tried to move, he pushed down on her back so she couldn't budge.

"It hurts Steve," she yelled. "Damn it, it hurts!"

He ignored her and kept pushing inside, deeper and deeper. Steve pushed past the point of resistance and was fully inside of her. Then he started pounding away. Not too sure of what she was feeling, but he was hitting something that was causing her extreme pain.

She tried to move away from him, but he held her down. She balled the sheets into her fist, clenched her teeth, buried her head into the mattress and cried, as Steve fucked her mercilessly.

"You. Talkin'. Bout. You. Ain't. Gonna. Give. Me. This. Ass. This. Is. My. Ass. Whose ass is this?"

She couldn't answer.

"Bitch, I said whose ass is this?"

He grabbed her hair, balling it into his fist, and yanked her head back.

"It's yours," she cried. "It's yours."

He continued holding her head back and fucked her harder and harder for thirty more seconds before he ejaculated inside her rectum.

Now she was sobbing uncontrollably. She couldn't help it. She was in the type of pain that she'd never felt before.

Steve collapsed on top of her, but he was still inside of her. He was breathing heavily and his sweat poured all over her back. Moments later, he got up and pulled himself out of her.

"Ouch," Nadia cried.

Steve went in the bathroom and took a shower. Her hemorrhoids were clearly hanging out of her rectum. She managed to get up and look in the mirror. It looked like she had two large keloids attached to her asshole.

She lay back on the bed, and her rectum was on fire. Her lower abdomen was hurting and her neck was sore. She felt like she had been in a fight.

Steve came out of the bathroom, looking mad as hell. "I can't believe your ass," he said. "You said you could take it for me and then you start crying and shit. Damn, how am I supposed to enjoy myself when my wife is acting like a bitch when I'm trying to make love to her?"

Nadia said nothing. What could she say? She had let him down.

"That bullshit meant nothing to me," he continued. "I had been looking forward to seeing you all day and you fuck my day up like this!"

Steve grabbed a pair of sweats from the closet and stormed out of the bedroom. Several minutes later, the front door slammed.

I want to die. I want to die. I want to die. I'm a failure. I'm a loser. I can't do shit right.

Nadia painfully crawled under the blanket and curled up. This was the darkest time of her life.

Chapter 20

Nadia barely slept through the night, waking up every so often, crying herself back to sleep. Going to the bathroom was a nightmare, as her bottom was intensely sore and her rectum was swollen. Because she endured immense pain just sitting down, let alone trying to have a bowel movement, she urinated while taking a shower.

From somewhere unknown, she mustered the energy to dress for work. Steve was sleeping on the couch. She took his key off of his chain and replaced it with hers so he could take her car to get it serviced. She opened the door slowly, walked out and closed it quietly. She didn't want to wake him. It's no telling what he would have said to her this morning.

When Nadia started the ignition, Miles Jay's CD filled the car. She backed out of the driveway and headed for work. Steve's car was very clean and it rode smooth, too. *I should drive this car more often,* she thought, as she grooved to Miles Jay and pulled up to her school.

Automatically today was going to be an extremely busy day for Nadia, since visitors from the Board of Education were expected next week, the school had to be in order. She didn't even see Theresa or Mr. Lowe, guessing they had to get their paperwork, classrooms, etcetera, together, too. She worked all day and realized that when she stayed busy, her mind didn't linger on the negativity in her life.

The day passed by rather quickly, but Nadia was disappointed, as it meant that she had to go home. As she packed up her things and checked her cell phone, she saw that Steve had called sixteen times. *"Nadia, I need my car today. I will take your car tomorrow. I promise. Call me back."*

What was the urgency?

After huffing and puffing at the idea of Steve calling her phone sixteen times, she left school and headed for the car. Once inside, she tried calling him a few times, but he didn't answer. Shrugging, she put the phone down on the passenger's seat, started the car and pulled out of the school's parking lot.

At the traffic light, she thought about her life at home and how miserable it was and how Steve wasn't shit. Deep in her thoughts, her foot slipped off the brake and her car eased into oncoming traffic. Startled, she yelled, "Oh shit!" and slammed on the brakes. She heard a thump under her feet, but ignoring it, she quickly put the car in reverse, looked in the rearview mirror, and backed out of traffic. Her heart was pounding and she could barely catch her breath. Reverting to the thump she'd heard under her foot, she looked down. It was a cell phone. She looked on the passenger seat. Her phone had not budged. As she reached for the phone, a car behind her honked its horn. Looking up, Nadia saw that the light was green. She'd worry about it later.

When she came to the shopping mall at the next intersection, she pulled in and parked. Without reluctance, she picked up the unknown cell phone and turned it on. Her heart was beating a mile a minute. She looked through the call log and saw *Wifey* multiple times. But, *Wifey's* number wasn't her phone number. *What in the hell?*

Wifey and her husband had been talking for several months. Now, it felt like her heart was moving at warp speed, and she literally had to take a deep breath and gain her composure.

Her cell phone started ringing and it was Steve. She ignored it.

As she browsed the photo gallery, her mouth fell open. Pictures of Karen stared back at her. There was a picture of her licking her nipples. There was a picture of her playing in her vagina. There was a picture of her with panties that read: "Steve's Pussy" across the front. There was a picture of her with her legs spread wide open. Then, there were just casual pictures of her that she sent to him randomly.

Nadia's vision became blurred by tears. *What about this can't I really believe? Don't I know this shit already?*

Enduring more torture, she scrolled through the text messages. Her cell phone was still ringing. It was still Steve and she still didn't answer it.

She couldn't believe the numerous texts between the two of them. Before she started reading, she got out of the car and stretched. She walked into the drug store and bought a soda and a bag of chips. She was hungry and knew she would be sitting there for a while.

10:02 AM Wifey: Babe you don't know how bad I wish I would've met you first. I hate it here and I'm so unhappy. The only thing that gives me any happiness is when I talk to you every day.

10:24 AM Steve: I know what you mean. I've been living with this old hag for a few years now. I have to be here with her for the kids, but baby I swear if I could get away from her I would.

10:33 AM Wifey: Why didn't you approach me first at the bar? My life could've been so different.

"Oh yeah," she said out loud. "Steve was married at the bar and it hasn't seemed to change anything." She grabbed a chip, took a sip and kept reading. Looking at the word *Wifey* on every text was killing her.

10:35 AM Steve: I wanted you bad baby. You saw how I was looking at you. I think your hater husband saw it too, that's why he couldn't wait to announce that I was married. Lol.

10:42 AM Wifey: He can be such a bitch sometimes. Lol.

10:51 AM Steve: I grew up with him. I know that better than anybody. Lmao.

The next day.

4:43 AM Steve: Good morning Baby.

Damn, he was sending her texts from the house first thing in the morning.

4:45 AM Wifey: Good morning Luv

4:50 AM Steve: Have a good day today. Think about me.

4:52 AM Wifey: I can't think of anything else. Luv u.

4:55 AM Steve: Luv u too.

"Luv u too," she said out loud. She couldn't remember the last time Steve told her that he loved her. It was too painful, and she wanted to take that fucking phone and throw it out the window, but she couldn't do that. She kept reading.

10:52 AM Steve: Hey baby. I'm missing you right now.

10:56 AM Wifey: Baby I miss you too. I'm so glad you just hit me. I was getting ready to go off up in here. These people are getting on my damn nerves.

11:02 AM Steve: Don't let them take you there beautiful. Think about me when you get mad at them and see what happens. Lol

11:09 AM Wifey: See, that's why you're my boo. I feel better already.

11:10 AM Steve: That's what I'm here for.

11:16 AM Wifey: It's almost lunch time. I'm starving.

11:18 AM Steve: I have something you can eat on.

11:20 AM Wifey: And I can't wait! I already know it's gonna taste so good.

11:23 AM Steve: I can't wait either. It's gonna be just me and you finally. I get to have you all to myself. What you gonna wear?

11:26 AM Wifey: I'm not telling you. It's gonna be something special for my man.

"Your man!" she shouted. "Who the fuck is your man?" A woman getting in her car next to her was staring at her. She didn't care. If she were reading this shit about her husband, she'd be screaming at the phone, too.

> *11:30 AM Steve: Damn baby. You got me hard as shit over here just thinking about what your sexy ass gon be wearing.*

> *11:31 AM Wifey: I feel better at this job already knowing I'm gonna be in your arms soon. I can't wait to get some good loving. Where are we going?*

> *11:33 AM Steve: Don't you worry about that. My lady just better be ready to be surprised.*

"Your lady? You call that raggedy bitch a lady!" she screamed at the phone.

> *11:35 AM Wifey: I can't wait. I'm getting all juicy between my legs just thinking about making love to you.*

> *11:38 AM Steve: My dick is swelling up right now. You got me at work with my dick sitting straight up in my pants.*

11:40 AM Wifey: Don't let anybody see my dick and get all excited. I might have to hurt you. Some bitch might be looking at you and then I'm gonna have to come down there.

11:42 AM Steve: Calm down baby. This belongs to you. If my trifling ass wife ain't getting it you know nobody else can get it.

"I don't want your slimy dick," she yelled. "And you force it on me!"

Nadia sat the phone down for a minute. She had to try to digest what she was reading. She reclined the seat and closed her eyes. Steve was still calling her phone. She looked at his name on the LCD screen. *Who is this man that I married?*

After a few moments, she picked up Steve's phone, took a deep breath and continued reading.

11:46 AM Wifey: So what you're telling me is that you don't sleep with Nadia.

11:50 AM Steve: Fuck no. I don't want it. She tries but I push her ass away. All I want is you. The thought of her makes my dick limp as hell. But when I think about you my shit stays hard like it is right now. Lol.

11:52 AM: Wifey: It's the same with Malik. He tried to kiss me and touch me last night, but I just walked away from him.

11:55 AM: Steve: You better not let him touch you. I mean that shit.

11:56 AM: Wifey: Didn't I tell you that this is your pussy.

11:58 AM: Steve: You just don't want my dick to go down do you? Lol

12:03 PM: Wifey: When I see that thang I'm putting my stamp on it.

12:05 PM: Steve: My dick has had Karen stamped on it for a long time.

12:08 PM: Wifey: Oh, I likes that shit. Lol. I have a lunch meeting at 12:15. I will hit you as soon as it's over. Luv u.

12:10 PM: Steve: Luv u too baby.

12:13 PM Steve: Take this piece of meat with you to lunch.

Attached to the text was a picture of Steve's penis. He must've gone into the bathroom and snapped the picture quickly because from the top angle, his penis stood straight up, his pants down around his ankles, covering his shoes and the tile on the bathroom floor.

"That motherfucking bastard!"

She had to take another short break. She rested her head on the steering wheel. She was hurting so bad and she didn't know how much more she could take. But she couldn't stop reading. She had to know everything. Malik and Steve had been best friends since childhood. Out of all the women on Earth, he had to choose his best friend's wife. Why?

Nadia thought back to the time Steve came in the house telling her everything that Karen said to him about Malik. She was getting ready to let those thoughts invade her mind and then she had to stop them. There was shit in front of her that had a tight grasp on her attention.

She picked up the phone and then it hit her. How did he get this fucking phone and how was he paying the bill? She knew what bill he wasn't paying, the damn daycare.

> *12:15 PM Wifey: Damn baby you almost made me drop my phone. I'm on my way out now but I am definitely gonna be thinking on how to marinate on this meat!*

2:05 PM Wifey: You messed my head up with that pic baby. Lol I don't even know what the meeting was about. I just kept thinking about sliding on your dick. I'm wet as shit right now.

2:21 PM Steve: And I can't wait to feel that wet pussy. Baby my reservations for the room got fucked up. Now I can't get a room at the hotel that I wanted. How you feel about coming to my house in the morning? If you're not comfortable with it I understand and I can try to get us a room somewhere else.

2:26 PM Wifey: What about Nadia? I'm not trying to get caught in your house.

2:33 PM Steve: Nadia's not a problem. I will just get up in the morning like I'm doing my normal routine and back track. She never calls me at work anyway and if she calls my cell you just be quiet.

2:35 PM Wifey: Sounds good to me. I can't wait.

2:41 PM Steve: I'm gonna tell Nadia I can't pick up Darryl. That will give us a little extra time.

2:44 PM Wifey: Yes baby I'm so excited. It makes me feel good to see my man do whatever he has to do to spend time with me. I'm so ready to make love to you.

2:52 PM Steve: I'm ready too baby. I will have everything together for you. Don't worry about eating. Daddy gonna feed you.

3:01 PM Wifey: You just really made my day. What time should I be there?

3:08 PM Steve: I was just thinking. Can you drive to your job and I can pick you up? I don't think Nadia will come home but just in case something strange happens it won't look crazy if just my car is here.

3:10 PM Wifey: Yeah I didn't think about that. Ok, I can do that. What time are you coming because I already took off for tomorrow? I just want to be able to go from my car to yours.

3: 13 PM Steve: Get up and act like you're going to work like I am. Just make it seem like any old day.

I married one sneaky motherfucker! Nadia thought, fuming!

3:15 PM Wifey: I am. Malik calls me at work though so I told him I would be in conferences all day long. Damn, what you said is a good idea because my car will still be at work! My baby is smart as hell!

3:22 PM Steve: And my baby is fine as shit and smart enough to know she has a smart man. Lol

3:25 PM Wifey: Exactly. I'm getting out of here in about five minutes or so. If you can get away even for a few minutes around 7 call me. The other phone will be on but I'm turning it off at 7:30. I would love to just hear your voice even if it's for a few seconds.

3:26 PM Steve: I will try my best baby. But if I can't I will see your beautiful face first thing in the morning. I will be there at exactly 8.

3:28 PM Wifey: And I will be in your car at 8:01! Try to call me tonight. Luv u.

3:29 PM Steve: Luv u too baby.

How I'm able to sit here and take this I will never know, she thought, as she checked Steve's phone records. Sure enough, he called her at seven o'clock on the dot and they talked until seven twenty-six.

"I guess that was why he was always getting mad and leaving out of the house,"

She returned to the texts.

> *7:57 AM Steve: I'm here waiting. Later.*
>
> *7:58 AM Wifey: I'm pulling up now.*
>
> *5:02 PM Wifey: I miss you already.*
>
> *5:05 PM Steve: I miss you too baby. After today I don't even want to look at my wife. Look at this pic I took of her ugly ass. Now you see why I want to be with you?*

Steve had taken a picture of Nadia when she was sleeping with a tear-stained face. Just looking at that picture showed her all of the hurt she endured even in her sleep.

> *5:07 PM Wifey: That's what I'm talking about. Damn she looks fucked up. Lol You know I don't want Malik anywhere near me. I'm gonna have to make something up to keep him away. Lol*

5:09 PM Steve: You better keep his ass away. That shit's mine!

5:12 PM Wifey: French toast and bacon for breakfast! Steak and rice for lunch! You did it up for me. I can't stop thinking about how much I love you.

"He cooked!" She was shaking as she kept reading.

5:14 PM Steve: You're my princess.

5:15 PM Wifey: And you made me feel like one. That sponge, bubble bath was so romantic. Rose petals and all. Candles and soft music. I'm so giddy right now. I wish I could just be with you right now. I need some more of those soft kisses.

5:16 PM Steve: Baby don't make me think about those lips right now. You're gonna get my dick started all over again. Now I can't stop thinking about how those lips looked around my dick and those pretty little noises you were making while you were sucking on it. Damn girl.

5:17 PM Wifey: And I can't stop thinking about how you made love to my pussy with your mouth. You made me cum so hard.

Disgusted, she threw the phone down on the passenger side floor and jumped out of the car. She wasn't sure where she was going or what she was doing, but she needed some air. *My husband ate another woman's pussy? His best friend's wife's pussy!* She walked back into the drug store for no particular reason other than she had to walk around.

To the customers, she looked like a crazed woman, pacing up and down the aisles, crying uncontrollably. She stopped in the aisle with the deodorants and lotions and cradled her face in her palms. Grief overtook her at that moment and she couldn't contain it any longer; too hurt to be embarrassed. No one in the store existed. Only Nadia and her pain.

She felt a gentle tap on the shoulder. Two elderly, black women were standing beside her. They looked to be in their mid-seventies.

"Young lady, if it didn't kill you then you can make it," said the first elderly lady. "You believe in God?"

"Yes ma'am," she said. She was always taught to respect her elders.

"Then let Him handle it. Let me ask you something. Is whatever you're crying about too big for the God you serve?"

"No ma'am, it isn't," she said, but wondering how much she really believed it at that point. Her pain seemed unbearable and unfair.

"I don't even know what your problem is," said the second elderly woman. "But I'm going to praise God for you that you're going through it. He brought you to this breaking point to teach you something. You better bless His name in this rain so that He can bring you the sunshine."

She looked at them through blood shot eyes. "Thank you both so much." She started to cry again. "Thank you."

"Trust God even in this," said the first elderly lady. "Get this in your spirit. Yea though I walk through the valley of the shadow of death, I will fear no evil. I will fear no evil. I will fear no evil. For thou art with me. Now young lady, go forth and live! The Lord is with you."

"Girl don't you start nothing in this here store," said the second elderly lady. "We be done had church up in here!"

They all laughed, which was what Nadia needed at that moment. A good laugh, despite the pain that encompassed her.

The women gave her hugs and just like that, they were gone.

"Thank you God," she said, as she walked out of the store back to the car.

Simply amazing, she thought. Had she gotten out of the car a second earlier or a second later, she wouldn't have run into those two angels. Truly, God was with her.

When she got in her car, she looked at her cell phone. Steve was calling like crazy. It was a little after five. She left work two hours ago. She picked up Steve's phone and couldn't believe her eyes.

5:06 PM Wifey: Hey Baby! I miss you.

"She just sent this shit!" She was yelling at the phone. She wanted to respond, but she had to keep reading about what happened at her house first.

> *5:19 PM Steve: Your juices tasted so fucking sweet. I tried to get every drop. Damn you were so wet. You have the fattest, wettest pussy. No wonder I'm so in love with your sexy ass.*

> *5:22 PM Wifey: Thank you baby. I feel so much closer to you now that we're not using condoms anymore.*

> *5:24 PM Steve: Yeah you can't get caught if there are no wrappers. Didn't want to take any chances on messing up our new daytime vacation spot.*

She threw the phone down, again. *I better stop doing that before I break it*, she thought. She picked it up, took another deep breath and kept reading.

> *5:26 PM Wifey: You felt so good inside of me baby. I can't stop thinking about it.*

> *5:28 PM Steve: My dick is so hard right now.*

> *5:29 PM Wifey: I wish I could be all over that thing right now.*

5:31 PM Steve: Me too baby. But in a little while we will do this again, I promise.

5:32 PM Wifey: Make sure you tell Nadia her bed sleeps well! Lol.

5:34 PM Steve: Lol! Now that's funny.

5:36 PM Wifey: Just curious babe. Did you change the sheets?

5:40 PM Steve: Hell no. I'm gonna let her dumb ass sleep in your pussy juice! Lol!

Speechless, she was completely numb. She cried some more. *He had her in my tub and in my bed. Then why was I so surprised when I let him say her name while he was fucking me?*

5:43 PM Wifey: Now that's funny! Lol Oh and thank you for the $200. I wanted to spoil myself a little bit and my baby came through for me. I love you so much.

5:45 PM Steve: Anything for my love.

"Wait a fucking minute! One thousand forty dollars that they took out of my account. Steve didn't pay for shit! I did!"

Enraged, she kept reading.

5:47 PM Wifey: I'm pulling up to the house now baby. Thank you and I'm gonna think about you all night.

5:49 PM Steve: I've already started thinking about you and my dick has too. Lol. Ok baby I love you.

5:50 PM Wifey: I love you too. Kisses!

The tears came again. She stopped looking at the texts and tried to check his voicemail messages, but she didn't have his code. She wanted to know it all. And, her phone was still ringing. The text messages had started up again a few days later. She couldn't make out why there were no texts between those days, but when she looked at the call log, there were calls during the time they weren't texting. *Son of a bitch!*

4:45 AM Steve: Good morning Luv

4:47 AM Wifey: Good morning Baby

4:50 AM Steve: Think of me today.

4:53 AM Wifey: You're late, I already am.

8:19 AM Wifey: I'm sitting here and I hate being away from you. I just want to see you so bad.

9:02 AM Steve: I want to see you too baby. This is just a rough week.

9:10 AM Wifey: Make it happen baby.

9:16 AM Steve: I could invite you and Malik over this weekend. Lol

9:18 AM Wifey: Why don't you do that?

9:20 AM Steve: Baby, I was just joking. How would I do that?

9:33 AM Wifey: I don't know but it would be exciting. They don't know what's going on and we could just play around and be doing our little thing and they wouldn't have a clue. How's that sounding to you baby?

9:36 AM Steve: Exciting as shit. Now you got me thinking. I love this kind of shit.

9:40 AM Wifey: Just do what you said. Invite Malik and I over. I have a meeting at 9:45 so think

194 | *Nicole McKay*

on it and I will hit you after I get out of the meeting. Luv u.

9:42 AM Steve: I love your sexy, sneaky ass too!

1:07 PM Wifey: We just got out of the meeting and our team leader treated us to lunch today.

1:21 PM Steve: Who that dude Thomas? Don't make me come up there and whip his ass.

1: 24 PM Wifey: I told you that you don't have anything to worry about with him. All I want is you. So what did you come up with?

1:26 PM Steve: I don't want you going to lunch with that man anymore, I don't care what it is. You got that?

1:28 PM Wifey: Okay baby, I'm sorry. I got it. I will make sure that doesn't happen again.

My husband is getting jealous over his best friend's wife having lunch with another man? She wiped the tears, swallowed hard and kept reading.

1:30 PM Steve: I'm going to tell Nadia that you and Malik are having problems and I want y'all to come over. How's that sound?

1:32 PM Wifey: Sounds good to me. I don't care what you tell her as long as I see you.

1:38 PM Steve: And I just want you to know that everything that is prepared to eat on that day is from me to you. It'll be my way of spoiling you in front of them. That's what I was thinking on while you were having lunch with that other man.

1:40 PM Wifey: I told you that won't happen again. And I love you that much more for spoiling me.

1:42 PM Steve: I want you to wear something special for daddy.

1:45 PM Wifey: Well thanks to my boo, I have a little extra money. So, I will go out and find something and you know that whatever I'm wearing is just for you. How does that sound? Lol

1:49 PM Steve: Sounds like my baby's a winner.

1:51 PM Wifey: We have a 2:00 meeting and it's gonna last through the end of the day. If you can, call me at 7. I can't wait until this weekend.

1:53 PM Steve: Don't say anything to Malik. I will suggest to him that y'all come over just to chill.

1:55 PM Wifey: This gets better and better. Do what you do daddy! I won't say anything to him. Luv u.

1:56 PM Steve: Luv u too baby.

She scrolled through the texts, which were more of the same. They seemed to text almost every day. This was unbelievable to her. Nadia was now getting a thrill out of Steve calling her phone back to back. She read and read until she came to an argument between the two of them. She thought the shock value of it all had worn off, but it hadn't.

8:10 AM Wifey: You couldn't tell me good morning today?

9:33 AM Steve: For what? Let that nigga you live with tell you good morning.

9:34 AM Wifey: I know you're not mad at me.

9:40 AM Steve: You kissed him in front of me.

9:43 AM Wifey: That kiss wasn't for him, it was for you. I just wanted you to watch me and think about us. I thought you knew that. You kissed your wife too and sucked her damn titty.

9:45 AM Steve: Shit what the fuck else was I supposed to do? If I didn't do that I would've slapped the shit out of you. Plus you said you don't fuck him.

10:02 AM Wifey: You said you don't fuck her! I knew your ass was lying.

10:05 AM Steve: You let that nigga fuck you in the ass! You the fucking liar bitch!

10:07 AM Wifey: Steve don't be like that. You know that I love you. I didn't know you would act like this. You even tasted my nipple for a few seconds in the bathroom. I don't care nothing about him. All I care about is you. I was just scared to tell you the truth because I don't want to lose you. Please don't leave me baby.

10:10 AM Steve: I don't even know how I can talk to him anymore knowing he's fucking you a couple of nights a week. This shit hurts babe.

10:11 AM Wifey: But when I'm with him I swear all I'm thinking about is you. I need those morning texts. It gives me something to look forward to. Trust me, I love you.

10:15 AM Steve: I'm going for a walk. I gotta think about some things.

10:16 AM Wifey: Baby you're scaring me. Please don't do this to me.

There were no more texts from Steve. Just pleading texts from Karen and the one that she just sent. Nadia decided to respond.

6:56 PM Steve: Look I decided I love my wife. You're a trifling bitch and you need to leave me the fuck alone. Dealing with you was the biggest mistake of my life and I'm going to make things right with my family. I got what I needed from you and now you're useless. And your pussy stinks!

Nadia looked at the clock and a few hours had passed. Steve had called her at least twenty more times. He had to know something was wrong. He had to know that she found his phone.

Nadia had Malik's phone number stored in her phone. It took her about two hours, but she forwarded Malik and herself every single text and picture that was on Steve's phone. Then Nadia deleted the texts that she sent, so that Steve wouldn't realize she read the messages. She put the phone back under the driver's seat.

Nadia headed home.

Chapter 21

As Nadia pulled up in front of her home, Steve was standing on the front porch looking frantic. Nonchalantly, she grabbed her things out of his car, closed the door and sashayed toward him.

"Where the hell have you been? I've been calling you all day."

She walked past him and into the house.

Steve walked behind her and snatched his keys from her. He went out to the car and seemed to be happy with his findings. Infuriated, he stormed into the house.

"You hear me talking to you?" Steve's phone started ringing. "Shit, it's Malik. I'll call him in a minute." Steve walked toward her. "Bitch…"

And then she lost it!

Nadia cocked back and hit that asshole with everything she had. She shocked herself when she connected, but something inside her wouldn't let up.

Her ass was on fire! He took her money, he raped her, he disrespected her, he was fucking around on her…it all just came to a head.

Steve tried to grab her, but he couldn't hold her. She was a woman gone wild; the shock of it all was too much for him, too. He released his grip and walked away, but he wasn't getting away that easily. She charged toward him, jumped on his back and pushed him to the floor. It felt like she was having an outer body experience, as she swung wildly and hit Steve in the mouth. She saw blood. He became enraged, jumped up and hit her in the neck. She charged toward him and he pushed her back. She fell, but got up and charged at him with such force that they both crashed to the floor.

"You bastard!" she yelled, throwing some mighty powerful punches. "You slimy motherfucker!"

With each punch, she felt a release. She was going for blood and she wanted his!

He tried to get up, but she wouldn't let him, as they rolled around on the living room floor. She kept pushing and punching. How she kept this man down, she will never know, but looking at his face pissed her off, and there was pleasure in knowing that she destroyed his smile.

Realizing his front tooth dangled from his mouth, he became more enraged and smacked her in the face so hard, her neck twisted around like the Exorcist.

That pissed her off more. Lalah Ali had nothing on Nadia, as she was too fired up to feel any of his blows. She grabbed his neck and started choking the shit out of him. She was choking him and banging his head against the floor. He was gasping for air and she squeezed tighter. "Die, motherfucker, die!" she chanted repeatedly. He was hitting her in the head, as she was choking him, but she refused to let go!

Steve's eyes bugged out of his head as Malik burst through the door.

Malik picked her up off him. She was kicking and screaming and trying to twist from Malik's grasp. Malik pulled her into the kitchen. She tried to run out, but he pushed her back in and ran toward Steve who was still on the floor gasping.

"My wife, nigga? My wife? You were fucking my wife?" Malik said through tears. Then he kicked the hell out of Steve's chest. Steve hid his face as Malik stomped the shit out of him. This went on until Malik slumped down beside Steve in exhaustion and started crying.

Nadia walked past the two of them, grabbed her keys and purse, got in her car and left. Driving erratically, she realized she had to get somewhere and calm down. She pulled into the nearest gas station and started crying. She looked at herself in the rearview mirror and at the long scratch down her right cheek. Her right eye looked bloodshot. She also had a terrible pain in her neck, and her chest ached horribly.

She sat idle for fifteen minutes, thinking of nothing in particular. Her mind was gone. She didn't want to think. She didn't want to talk. She didn't want to do anything, but sit and stare. She gathered the energy to start the car and realized she was heading toward Theresa's house. She looked a hot mess, but it didn't matter. Today her life had changed.

As soon as Theresa opened the door, Nadia fell into her arms.

Without a word, Theresa led her into the house, sat her on the couch and helped her undress; removing her bloodstained clothes, and wrapped her in the faux fur that was accenting the couch.

"You want to take a shower?"

Nadia shook her head.

Theresa got a hot washcloth and gently wiped Nadia's face and hands. Tears were flowing from her eyes, too, but she didn't ask any questions.

"I'll be right back," she said. Moments later Theresa returned with a nightgown, a pillow and a blanket.

Nadia stared at her.

She helped her put on the nightgown. Then she lifted her feet up on the couch and propped her back up on the pillow.

Theresa sat next to her, hugging her. Nadia hugged her back and she couldn't let go. She held Theresa for all of her pain. She buried her face in her best friend's neck and released every tear within her. Nadia cried for Nadia. Nadia cried for her children. Nadia cried for her life.

Chapter 22

When Nadia woke up in the middle of the night, she had no idea where she was. Then, she remembered she was on Theresa's couch. The events from the previous day haunted her, as she cried some more. She had to use the bathroom, but when she tried to stand up every muscle in her body ached.

"Let me help you," Theresa said.

Theresa was wrapped in a blanket sleeping on the floor beside the couch. She helped Nadia up, but she hurt so badly that she couldn't move for several minutes. Theresa walked with her very slowly to the bathroom and helped her to the toilet. The best feeling was releasing that urine. She couldn't even wipe herself. Theresa was one hell of a friend because she took that tissue and wiped Nadia's grown behind. And, she was in too much pain to be embarrassed. She just needed help.

Theresa still had tears in her eyes. When Nadia stood to wash her hands, she understood why. The right side of her face was swollen and blackened. Theresa tried to usher her out of the bathroom, but she wouldn't budge. She had to look at herself. That person in the mirror wasn't Nadia. She hadn't come into her marriage busted up. Looking at her face and feeling the physical pain was more than she could bear. It was the result of an abusive journey. But she was alive and she was going to live.

Theresa helped her out of the bathroom and into her bedroom. Still no words were spoken between them, and Nadia was glad to be getting in the bed. Theresa hoisted her up a little and she cringed from pain. Theresa moved the pillows and she was able to rest on her side. Theresa then pulled the blankets over her, adjusted her down pillow and left the room.

Lying there, Nadia started thinking about the text messages. With the way Steve was on her about sex, she just didn't think that he was actually penetrating another woman. She figured he might flirt, but what kind of a pervert was this monster? She didn't even know who he was. More than that, she didn't know who she was.

She still couldn't believe she fought Steve. Who was that person that threw those punches? *Damn it, it was me!* That thought made her smile because she knew she had hurt him. She didn't have a clue what happened when she left Steve and Malik in the house, but she wondered if she was going to be a widow before she would be divorced.

Finally, she drifted off to sleep. And this time, she wasn't in the fetal position.

Nadia slept until noon, which was unusual for her. When she opened her eyes, Theresa and Mr. Lowe were standing over her.

Theresa had an ice pack for her face. She gently placed it on the swelling.

Mr. Lowe sat down on the bed. "This may sound like a crazy question, but how are you feeling?"

"I don't know," Nadia said.

"When you're ready, we can talk," Theresa interjected. "Don't worry about anything. I called in for us and Mr. Lowe took off to come and check on you. I called him last night after you fell asleep on the couch."

"Thank you."

Mr. Lowe handed Nadia the pain relievers and the water from the nightstand. He helped her to sit up. He put the glass of water to her lips and she popped the pain pills. It pained her to swallow.

"I have so much to tell y'all," she managed to say.

"Do you want to talk now?" Theresa asked.

Nadia did. "Yes."

"Are you hungry? I can make you something to eat first."

"No, I don't think that I can chew on my right side. And right now, I just don't have an appetite."

"Nadia, you better tell me something soon. I'm about ready to ride to your house and beat this dude down!"

"Okay. It's a long story. Get comfy."

Theresa sat on the other side of her and Mr. Lowe positioned himself at her feet after he propped her up on the pillows. She began telling them the whole story. She left no stone unturned.

Nadia asked Theresa to get her cell phone from her purse. Nadia pulled up the forwarded texts. Mr. Lowe sat next to her and they read through each of them.

Steve called four times while they were reading.

"Nadia let me answer this phone," Mr. Lowe said. "Please! If for no other reason just to let him hear another man on the other end."

"But what will that do?" Nadia asked.

"Nothing, but make him feel like shit."

"I'm so sorry all of this had to happen to you," Theresa said.

"I'm not," Mr. Lowe said. "Now you know and believe it or not, you're already better for it. And now that I know the whole story, you look pretty good to have fought a man!"

"You're right," Theresa said through laughter and tears.

"You know what?" Mr. Lowe said. "I have a great deal of respect for you right now. Although you endured a lot, you sought out our help. And you fought back. So many women go through this type of abuse, justify it and stay. You're strong, girl."

"He's so right," Theresa said, still looking through the phone. "I just can't believe what I'm reading. Steve has no conscience. He doesn't care who he hurts, as long as he gets what he wants."

"I love your response to Karen's ass though," Mr. Lowe said, cracking up. "You fucked her head up with that one."

"Yeah, but she probably ain't busted up like I am."

"Who knows?" Theresa said. "But if she's not busted up on the outside, she's definitely busted up on the inside. Your physical wounds will heal a whole lot quicker than her inner wounds. Her heart is broken, her marriage is probably over and it hit her from nowhere like a bolt of lightning. She doesn't know the Steve that you know, but from these texts it seems like she was well on her way to getting a dose of who he really is."

"So what are you going to do?" Mr. Lowe asked.

Nadia wasn't sure, which is what scared her. The only thing she did know was that she was not going back to Steve. She had to think about herself. With everything that had been going on, with her lying in bed depressed, to all of this affair shit going on, she hadn't even talked to her babies.

"The first thing that I have to do is call my kids and tell my parents something. I just can't let my children see me like this. I'm having a hard enough time with all of this, but I can't put this on them. Not right now."

Theresa handed her the phone and she dialed her parents' number.

"Hey, Ma."

"Nadia, how are you doing, baby?"

"I'm okay, I guess."

"What's wrong?"

Nadia remained silent.

"Nadia, what's wrong?" Her mother held a hint of anxiety in her voice.

"Well, Ma, Steve and I are having some problems and I really need some time to think about what to do."

"Is it another woman?" her mother blatantly asked.

"I can't be sure," she lied. "I just know that something's not right."

"Well, what do you need?"

"I know that you and Daddy have had the kids for a few days now, but if it's not too much trouble, would you mind keeping them for a few more days please? I will make it up to y'all some kind of way for taking care of them for me." She started crying.

Theresa handed her a tissue.

"Don't cry, baby, and you don't have to make anything up to us. These are our grandchildren. Hell, I don't know what I did before I had these youngins. They keep me going and I love having them around me. You just take care of yourself and I will have them call you after we pick them up from school."

"Thank you and I love you."

"I love you, too, baby. Take it to God and let Him fix it."

"I will." They hung up.

Theresa and Mr. Lowe were looking at her.

"Ma said that she would keep the kids while I figured things out."

"Why didn't you tell your mother what really happened?" Mr. Lowe asked.

"My mother would take all of this on and probably have an anxiety attack or something. All she needs to know is that something is wrong in my marriage. In time, I will tell her everything, but I would worry more about her than myself if I let that happen. And if she saw me like this she would bust a blood vessel."

Steve was calling her again.

"You're going to have to face him at some point," Theresa said.

"Oh I will. I definitely will."

"You're welcome to stay here as long as you like," Theresa offered. "It's no problem at all."

After showing up at Theresa's door with no warning, her words eased Nadia, as she didn't want to burden her. She felt so much better after hearing that.

"Are you sure? I know that people offer out of pity sometimes and I don't want to invade your space."

"Well, how about I would be offended if you didn't stay here in your time of need. You don't want to offend me, do you?"

Nadia smiled. "No."

"So shut up, lay back, chill and let somebody do something for you for a change. Deal?"

"Deal."

"Well, Nadia, you know I've been trying to sell my home that's close to the school," Mr. Lowe said. "With the economy being the way it is, it's been a downhill battle. If you're seriously interested, I could rent it out to you with the option to buy. It's a nice place, three bedrooms, three baths and a finished basement. Actually, the house is paid for so anything that I get will be a profit. I just don't want to move back into it because I love my house that I'm in now. If you give it some serious thought it could be a win-win situation for both of us."

Things seemed to be happening so fast and she had to let it all sink in. Mentally, she had checked out of her marriage years ago. She thought she was supposed to feel devastated and in some ways, she did. But more than anything, she felt a sense of freedom. She was hurting so deeply on the inside, yet she had one foot out the door and she wasn't going back.

"Give it some serious thought," Mr. Lowe said.

"I'll take it."

"Wait a minute," he said. "Don't you at least want to see it?"

"Nope, I'm going on your word. This is a power move and I have to make it. I can't go back home, I'm not living with my parents and I can't sit in limbo until something happens. So, I'll take it."

"See what I'm saying," Mr. Lowe said. "You're strong, Nadia. Stronger than you know."

Chapter 23

The following week, Nadia took off from work. Each day she got stronger and each day Steve called at least fifteen times. The swelling had gone down some in her face, but her neck was still sore and she was still kind of achy. Theresa was kind enough to sleep on the couch, offering her comfortable bed to Nadia. She wore Theresa's clothes and Theresa went out and got her everything she needed. She couldn't have asked for a better friend at this time in her life.

On Thursday afternoon when Theresa returned from work, Nadia was sitting on the couch. She had cleaned up the bathroom, the kitchen, the living room and the dining room. She had to do something to show her how thankful she was for her hospitality.

"Hey, girl. You look so much better today," she said. "Everyone at work is asking about you, but Mr. Lowe and I are sticking with our flu story."

Nadia laughed.

"Well, girl, I have to go home. I have to face Steve. It's time to let him know what I'm going to be doing and then do it. Mr. Lowe said I can be in his place on Monday, so if it's okay with you, can I stay here until then?"

"Uh…of course, you can," Theresa said with much concern. "Are you sure you want to go home? Do you want me to come with you?"

"No. I'm not scared. He can't do anything else to me. I just have to get this over with so I can move on. You know I never thought my life would turn out like this. My whole life changed within a matter of days. My biggest concern is not Steve, but explaining all of this to the kids. I guess that since we work with kids of divorced parents all the time, I know that they will be all right, eventually. I just don't look forward to their questions, sad faces and all of that stuff. At this point though, it doesn't even matter. I'm leaving, they're leaving and we will get through this together. But damn it, I'm not staying!"

"I'm so proud of you," Theresa said, hugging her. "Are you coming back here tonight?"

"Yes and when I get back I'm going to fix you dinner. You've been so wonderful to me and I want to repay you."

"You're gonna cook for little ol' me," Theresa said, batting her eyelashes and laughing.

"Yes, I'm cooking for little ol' you," she said and headed out of the door.

She got in her car for the first time since the night of the fight. There was blood on the steering wheel and a sick feeling came over her. She started questioning if going home was a good idea, but she couldn't disappoint herself. She had to face her fear. She had to face Steve.

As Nadia was heading toward the house, her cell phone rang. It was her parents' number.

"Hello."

"Hi, Mommy," Danielle said.

"Hey, baby!" she said crying, hoping Danielle wouldn't be able to tell.

"I miss you, Mommy. Grandma said you had to go out of town for your job. When are you coming back?"

Thank you, Ma!

"I'll be back next week. You having a good time?"

"Yep, Grandma gives us junk food all the time and Grandpa gets mad."

"Now don't you eat too much of that stuff, you hear me?"

"Yes, ma'am."

"Where is Darryl?"

"He's right here."

"Hello, Mommy."

"Hey, Darryl. Whatcha doin?"

"Mommy, on the way home I got an orange Corvette. I clicked it and its mine."

"Who cares," Danielle said in the background.

"I care, you doofus," he yelled back.

"Uh, Darryl, I love you."

"Love you, too, Mommy."

"Give Danny back the phone."

"Hi again, Mommy."

"I love you, Danny."

"I love you, Mommy. I will call you tomorrow."

"Okay, baby. Bye-bye."

"Bye."

Smiling, Nadia felt so much better after talking to the two who truly make up her world. She knew they were in good hands and it felt good to hear them arguing.

Steve had called twice when she was on the call with Darryl and Danielle. No need to call him back. She was going to see him.

When she pulled up to the house, his car was there. The car with the phone. The car with the phone with the messages. *I hate him, I hate him, I hate him.*

As she walked up the stairs toward the house, she felt braver than she ever has. However, she did have some anxiety, as she inserted the key into the lock, but that overwhelming fear that kept her imprisoned was gone.

Steve was occupying his usual seat on the couch, with his cell phone next to him. He was staring at a blank screen on the television. He looked like he had been in a fight with a bear. He had bandages around his ribs. His hand was wrapped in a bloody ace bandage. He had a huge knot over his left eye and he had one tooth hanging loosely in the front of his mouth.

"I've been calling you," he said. His voice was raspy and she had to strain to hear him.

"And I've been choosing not to answer."

He looked surprised by her comment, but then his face softened.

"I...I...I'm so sorry, baby," he said. "I don't know what came over me. I wasn't thinking right. You're a Christian, baby, and I know you can find it in your heart to forgive me."

"My Christianity isn't what's in question here."

Nadia looked around her house and thought of those text messages. She felt herself getting hot with anger. She walked to her room. It no longer felt like her room. Her bed had been defiled. Her bathroom, the place where she loved to soak, had been infiltrated by a big tittied bitch and that bum on the couch. Nothing about this place felt like home. She felt like a stranger invading someone else's home. This house is where her husband was going to entertain another woman any time he pleased.

She walked down the hall to the kitchen. There was a banana on the counter. She picked it up and walked back out to Steve. He had tears in his eyes. She didn't know how he got wrapped up and she didn't care enough to ask.

"Can you please forgive me, baby? Isn't that what your Bible says? Isn't that what you learn on Sundays? What kind of Christian are you if you can't forgive? I need you, and I need my kids."

She sat down on the couch across from him.

"My forgiveness of you is between me and my God. Don't pull that crap with me. Now you want to go to the Word? Well, can you tell me what the Word says about adultery?"

He said nothing.

"And you need me for what? You need me to fix your meals? You need me to clean the house? You need me to single handedly take care of the kids? You need me so you can take all of my money? Should I go on? What exactly do you need me for?"

"I'm sorry for all of that."

"And that's it? You're sorry. What are you sorry for? You're sorry for damn near ripping my ass apart? Huh? I should take this banana and ram it up your ass! Are you sorry for raping me? Or..."

"I never raped you!"

"You did, you good for nothing motherfucker! You did whatever you wanted to with my body! You fucked me silly damn near every day and you didn't care how I felt about it."

"But baby..."

"Shut up! I don't even know who you are. Every time I thought things couldn't get worse, they did. You don't give a damn about me or the kids."

"We can work this out," Steve pleaded. "Please, baby, don't be like that."

"Stop calling me baby. I'm not fucking *Wifey*. I'm the wife, but I'm really the chic on the side. Baby is your name for your best friend's wife, not me."

Steve looked away from her.

"And what kind of a friend are you? On the most basic level, you ain't shit. You don't care about nothing or nobody."

"Baby...I mean, Nadia, I do care about you."

"Well damn, I hate to see how you would treat me if you didn't."

There was silence for a few seconds. Steve finally spoke.

"Nadia, I don't know how to make this right. But I know that I can't be without you. Please give me another chance. All I want is my family. I don't know how I will make it without you. Please stay."

Steve looked so pitiful. Her heart ached and that pain began to resurface. There was a time when she loved this man. There was a time when she would do anything for him. There was also a time when this shit he was saying would've mattered, but today it didn't.

"Steve, you keep telling me what you need. Well, let me tell you what I don't need. I don't need a man who doesn't respect me. I don't need a man who abuses me. I don't need a man who gets a thrill out of watching me run around in circles for him. I don't need a man who steals money from me and I don't need a man who has no problem fucking his best friend's wife."

"I'm so sorry, Nadia. How can I make you believe me? I'm not going to deny any of what you're saying. I need help. Can you help me, Nadia, please? I need you."

"Steve, I gave you ten years of my life. That's damn near four thousand days. You couldn't determine in all of that time how to treat me or how to love me."

"I told you I need help…"

"Shut up. You had me for ten motherfucking years. You don't have one more day to hurt me. Today, your time has run out."

Steve tried to sit up, but the pain was too much for him. Tears started flowing from his eyes. Nadia got her purse and walked to the front door.

"Nadia, please don't go. I'm sorry. I love you."

"No you don't. You love Karen. You chose to tell her every day and you chose not to tell me."

"I didn't love her. I was....I just..." He couldn't say anything else.

"I'm done, Steve. This is over. I'm walking away from you and this. I can't be with you and I will never spend another day in this house. I don't know how the divorce process goes, but you best believe I'm getting ready to figure it out."

"Nadia, Nadia...."

The door closed behind her.

She could hear Steve screaming her name as she walked to her car.

"You okay?" she heard from across the street. It was Theresa and Mr. Lowe in Mr. Lowe's car, which was parked across the street.

"What are y'all doing here?"

"We were just making sure you were all right," Mr. Lowe yelled. "Follow us."

For the first time, Nadia felt like laughing, and she did. "Lead the way," she said, getting in her car.

She followed her friends. She followed the people who really loved her.

Chapter 24

Driving behind Theresa and Mr. Lowe gave Nadia time to reflect on Steve. *I'm really going to leave him.* She didn't know what the future held, but she knew who wouldn't be a part of it. She needed some healing for her soul, so she turned on the radio to the gospel station, and allowed the songs to minister to her spirit.

They pulled up to Mr. Lowe's vacant house, located only a few minutes from the school. Before they walked inside, Mr. Lowe looked at Nadia.

"Nadia, if you're serious, this can be your new home."

"I'm serious. Very serious."

Mr. Lowe gave her the key and they walked in. The place was beautiful. There were three floors. First, she walked up the spiral staircase. The master bedroom had a walk-in bathroom with a Jacuzzi and a marble sink. French doors opened to the balcony and a beautiful view of the trees. The other two bedrooms had large walk-in closets. Nadia walked back downstairs and into the kitchen, which had marble countertops and a beautiful stainless steel refrigerator and stove. The living room was overly spacious and the dining room was large enough for a conference room sized table.

"Mr. Lowe, this place is beautiful." Nadia was overjoyed. And, for a hot second, she had forgotten about the mess her life had become.

"It sure is," Theresa said.

"Let me show you the basement," Mr. Lowe said.

She walked downstairs and almost fainted. The basement was so wide, with a full bath, a full kitchen and the best part of all, a theatre room!

"Mr. Lowe, I can't believe this," she said, hugging him. "This seems too good to be true."

"Well, your credit is about to take a serious hit with you walking away from your house. So, to help you out, we are going to do the sell by owner process. That cuts out the middleman. You can rent first and then we can get the ball rolling for you to buy. You can stay here for the first three months, rent free, and then after that you can pay me seven hundred dollars a month. Financially, God has been good to me through the years and if I can bless someone else, especially a good friend who is trying to change her life, then I am going to do it."

Nadia was at a loss for words. God was blessing her and He was doing it swiftly.

"We love you," Theresa said.

"I love you guys, too."

"Can I stay here tonight?" Nadia asked.

"You can, but you don't have any furniture," Mr. Lowe said.

"That's okay. I just need to be here."

"Well, here are the keys. It's your place anyway. We will handle all of the paperwork and things like that sometime next week. Enjoy yourself, Nadia. Theresa, let's get out of here and let Nadia get used to her new home."

Theresa hugged Nadia. "God loves you, girl. His Word says to touch not His anointed. Steve learned that lesson the hard way."

Nadia nodded. "Thank you for all of your help and support. Oh, wait, I was supposed to cook you dinner tonight."

"That's okay. We will just have a huge house warming dinner over here and I will let you prepare me a few special dishes. Deal?"

"Deal, girl."

Theresa and Mr. Lowe hugged her one last time before leaving through the basement door.

When she woke this morning, Nadia had no idea she would be standing in her own place that night. What a difference a day makes. She knew she had some upcoming battles. The first would be explaining everything to her children in a way that they would understand. But her mind was made up and that was it. She also knew she was getting ready to go through a nasty divorce. She was ready for it all because now it was time for her to live.

She went to her purse and checked her phone. Steve called six times, and she had a text message from Malik.

4:36 PM Malik: I just want to thank you for letting me know what was going on. I tried to kick him to death but he wouldn't die. LOL I left Karen and moved in with my brother until I can figure things out. Glad we didn't have kids. I'm hurting but I can't be with her. I hope you are well. Call me when you can and we can talk about this whole thing. You're the real friend. Take care.

So, Malik left Karen. Well she can go back to my old house and live all she wants. Her stain is in the place anyway.

Nadia got on her knees in the middle of the basement floor and started to pray. She prayed for her mind. She prayed for her children. She prayed for Malik. She gritted her teeth and prayed for Karen. She dug even deeper and prayed for Steve and his relationship with his kids. She prayed for her parents. She prayed for her future with the kids in this new house. And, she prayed for God to help her to forgive everyone and move forward.

For years, she never understood why her life was so full of lows. From childhood molestations through being raped in her marriage and everything in between. Now, Nadia had reached a point of fearlessness and had finally taken control of her life. She had to take a journey of pain and ruthlessness to find her way. It was time for her to get reacquainted with Nadia, and truly learn who she really is. Steve, Karen, Malik and everyone in her life were a pivotal part of her journey. She broke away from the prison chains in her mind and freed herself. She was starting the second half of her life with a renewed mind and strength that she could only get from God. Now she understood the reason why.

ABOUT THE AUTHOR

Nicole McKay was raised in Hyattsville, Maryland. She graduated with a Bachelor of Arts in History and a Masters of Library Science from North Carolina Central University in Durham, North Carolina. God has blessed her with two beautiful children that bring her nothing but joy and happiness.

Nicole's mission is to help and inspire men and women through her work. She aspires to speak to the souls of people through her books and stage plays, and have them acknowledge and admit the truth, even when painful and difficult to conceive. She also sets out to let people know that no matter how tough and gut wrenching the situation may be, there's absolutely nothing under the sun that is too hard for God.

Nicole also wrote the sequel to *The Reason Why*, entitled, *More of the Same*.

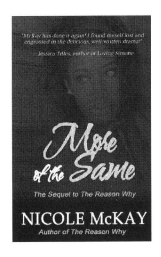

Made in the USA
Middletown, DE
12 March 2022

62356326R00135